Grimm Pursuit

Dogged Detectives, Volume 1

Izze Prin

Published by Grimm Tails Publishing, 2023.

GRIMM PURSUIT

First edition. May 12, 2023.

Copyright © 2023 Izze Prin.

ISBN: 979-8223296553

Written by Izze Prin.

Blurb

A DETECTIVE'S GRIEF and unwavering bond with her K-9 partner fuels a desperate pursuit to find two missing children.

Beth Danville, a seasoned detective haunted by personal tragedy, is in the peaceful town of Olympia, Washington, in search of solace. Still mourning the loss of her husband, she finds companionship and purpose in her faithful K-9 partner, Grimm, while they embark on an RV journey with no set destination. Together, they navigate the pain of the past and the uncertainty of the future.

When two young girls vanish under mysterious circumstances, Beth's life takes an unexpected turn. Drawn into the investigation alongside fellow detective Angela Rodriguez, she pushes the boundaries of her grief-stricken heart.

As Beth delves deeper into the case, she uncovers a web of secrets, deceit, and a twisted interpretation of salvation. With Grimm by her side, their unbreakable bond becomes a beacon of strength in the face of unimaginable evil. Beth's grief fuels her determination, transforming her into a relentless force that will stop at nothing to find two little girls before time runs out.

"Grimm Pursuit" is a captivating story of love, loss, and the extraordinary bond between a detective and her canine companion, where the pursuit of justice becomes a journey of healing and renewed purpose.

Chapter One

BETH GAZED OUT AT THE scenery, taking in the breathtaking view of the surrounding forest. The tall, thick trees swayed gently in the breeze, casting long shadows across the ground. The stream bubbled nearby, and the distant hoot of an owl added a contrasting note to nature's chorus.

Grimm bounded out of the RV and immediately started sniffing around, his nose to the ground as he explored the new surroundings. He trotted over to the stream, lapping up water with his tongue. Beth watched him for a moment, a smile tugging at the corners of her mouth. It was the little moments like this that made her appreciate her road trip with Grimm.

She took a deep breath of the crisp air, feeling a sense of calm wash over her. She loved being out in nature, away from the chaos of the city and the stresses of work. She and Grimm had a routine they followed when they set up camp, and she began to set up their home away from home. She pulled out their camping chairs and table and lit a lantern for light as the sun continued to set. Before it got dark, she started a small fire. She didn't feel like cooking in the confines of the small Class C, so she'd indulge in an unhealthy meal of hot dogs and marshmallows.

"Do you want a hot dog?"

Grimm looked at her with a head tilt and gave a low whine.

"I'll take that as a yes."

She entered the RV a moment later, overwhelmed with the memory of the day she and Joel picked it out. He'd been on leave from his latest deployment and had decided to retire. They'd planned to take an entire summer to travel, so they'd bought this RV after exploring their options.

Her gaze went to the bedroom at the back as she opened the fridge. They'd christened it well the first night of their first short trip. She ached to feel his arms around her and had to blink back tears. Meeting her hazel-eyed gaze in the chrome surface of the microwave above the stove, she pushed back her frizzy brown hair. "They wouldn't know me at work, baby," she said to Joel's picture, which she'd mounted on the wall. At work, she kept a short pixie cut to control her natural curls, but she'd let it grow during the last two months and hadn't bothered with much maintenance.

Grimm woofed at her and licked his lips, reminding her she had dinner to make. She reached down and ruffled the fur on his head. "Okay. I'm right behind you."

He spun and leapt from the RV, not bothering with the steps, as she followed behind. Once dinner was finished, they relaxed near the fire. Grimm laid by her feet, his nose twitching as he took in the scents of the surrounding forest. Beth pulled out her journal and started jotting down some notes about their trip so far, trying to get into the mindset of someone on vacation.

But the truth was, she was restless. Ever since Joel died, she had felt aimless, like she was wandering without purpose. She missed the adrenaline rush of solving cases and the camaraderie of her fellow detectives. She missed Joel most of all—the sound of his voice, his laughter, and his touch.

As she sat by the fire, lost in thought, her phone rang, jolting her out of her reverie. She reached for it, noticing the caller ID was from the department. She hesitated for a moment, unsure if she was ready to dive back into work so soon after Joel's death, but ultimately answered the call. "Danville," she said, trying to keep her voice steady.

"Beth, it's Cassia. I hate to do this to you, but we have a missing child case in Olympia. The parents are frantic, and the local police could use some extra help. Are you up for it?"

Beth took a deep breath, feeling a sense of purpose stir within her. She looked over at Grimm, who was staring up at her with his big brown eyes, as if he knew what was happening. "I'm in," she said, determination in her voice. "Give me the details, and I'll head out first thing in the morning."

Cassia gave her the details of the case, including the name of the missing child, Christa Stevens, and the address of her family's home in Olympia. Beth scribbled down notes in her journal, trying to organize her thoughts and plan her next steps.

After hanging up the phone, Beth sat back down by the fire, lost in thought once again. This case would be difficult, but she needed to take it on. She looked down at Grimm, who had nestled his head on her lap, as if offering comfort. "Looks like we're heading to Olympia, buddy," she said, scratching behind his ears. "Think you're up for the challenge?"

Grimm barked in response, wagging his tail as if to say he was ready for anything. Beth smiled. She was grieving, but she was still a detective and still capable of doing her job.

Beth and Grimm went back into the RV, and she started packing up their gear, getting ready for the journey ahead. Thinking about a missing child inevitably brought her thoughts to her own children—which she'd never have now that Joel was gone. She couldn't help but feel a sense of guilt as she thought about Joel's dream of starting a family. She wished she had made more time for him and their future together.

But right now, she needed to focus on finding Christa and bringing her home safely.

As she packed, she made a mental checklist of everything she would need for the case, including her badge and gun, her laptop, and her evidence kit. She made sure Grimm's vest was ready, and he had plenty of food and water. Once everything was in order, she climbed into bed and closed her eyes, trying to get some rest before the long day ahead.

She dreamt of Joel, of the life they had planned together. In her dream, Joel was there with her, holding her hand and laughing as they walked along a beach. The sun was shining, and the waves crashed gently against the shore. They talked about their future, about starting a family, and settling down. Beth was filled with happiness, and for a moment, everything felt perfect.

Then the dream shifted, and Joel was gone. She was standing alone on the beach, the waves crashing around her as she tried to call out for him. Panic rose within her, and she couldn't dispel the feeling of being alone and lost.

Suddenly, he touched her shoulder. She looked over at him, and a lump formed in her throat. "I thought you were gone."

He gave her a sad smile, and the wind blew his dirty blond hair into his eyes. He'd worn it longer and longer since leaving the Army. "I am, baby."

Even in her dream, it hit her like a gut punch. She bent forward to hold her stomach. "I miss you," she said, tears welling in her eyes.

Joel smiled at her, his gaze filled with love. "I miss you too, Beth, but you have to keep going. You have to keep doing what you were meant to do."

"I don't know if I can," she said, her voice cracking with emotion.

"You can," said Joel, taking her hand in his. "You're strong. Stronger than you realize."

Beth woke up, feeling that familiar loss and longing. She looked over at Joel's picture on her nightstand, and tears streamed down her face. She missed him so much, but she knew the dream version of him was her own subconscious telling her to keep going and keep fighting. Right now, that meant finding Christa and bringing her home. She wiped her tears away and got up, ready to face the day ahead.

She washed her face and brushed her teeth, trying to shake off the remnants of the dream. She dressed in her usual work clothes, a black suit and sensible shoes, and headed outside to start the RV. Grimm trotted out behind her, his tail wagging excitedly. She smiled at him, feeling a sense of comfort in his presence.

Once the RV started, she pulled out of the campsite and headed toward Olympia, her mind already racing with thoughts of the case. She thought about the Stevens family, wondering what they must be going through, and hoped she could bring them some peace by returning their child.

The RV rumbled along the highway, the scenery passing by in a blur. Beth tried to focus on the road, but her mind kept drifting back to Joel and their plans for the future. She needed to move on, but it was easier said than done.

Finally, she arrived in Olympia and pulled up to the Stevens' home. Protocol dictated she should go to the local station first, but it was vital to see the scene as quickly as possible. She took a deep breath, trying to steady her nerves, and climbed out of the RV. Grimm followed closely behind her, his nose twitching as he took in the new scents.

She approached the door and knocked. A woman with tear-streaked cheeks answered the door, with worry etched on her face. She introduced herself as Detective Danville and showed her badge, flashing it quickly since it was from Colorado. "I was hoping to hear more about Christa's disappearance.

"Of course." The woman, Greta Stevens, stepped aside to let Beth inside. The living room was tidy, with family photos on the mantel and a cat lounging on the sofa. Beth felt the oppressive weight of the situation as soon as she crossed the threshold.

"Please, come in," said Greta, gesturing to the sofa. "This is my wife, Lisa."

Lisa was sitting with her head in her hands, and she looked up as Beth entered. She was a beautiful woman with long, curly brown hair and bright green eyes that were now puffy and red from crying.

Beth sat down across from them and pulled out her notepad. "Can you tell me what happened?" she asked, hoping to get a better understanding of the situation.

Greta took a deep breath and began to speak. "Christa didn't come home from school yesterday. She always walks home, and we assumed she had gone to a friend's house or something. But when she didn't come home by dinner, we started to worry."

Lisa picked up the story. "We called her friends and her school, but no one had seen her. We called the police, but they said we had to wait twenty-four hours before filing a report. We couldn't wait that long, so we contacted the local news station, and they did a story on her. That's when the police started to take it seriously."

Beth nodded, assuming the story gone national, which was how Cassia had heard and asked her to get involved. She jotted down notes as she listened. "Do you have any idea where she might be?"

The couple shook their heads, and Lisa began to cry again. "We just want her home safely," she said.

Beth could feel the emotion in the room, and she hoped she could help bring Christa home. As she looked around the room, she noticed a cat lounging on the sofa. Grimm was sniffing around the cat, who was seemingly unbothered by his presence.

"Who's this?" she asked, gesturing to the cat.

"That's Rudolph," said Greta, smiling weakly. "He's Christa's cat."

Beth observed as Grimm sat down next to the cat and nudged him with his nose. Rudolph leaned into him, and Beth couldn't help but smile at the unexpected bond forming between the two animals.

She turned back to the couple, trying to be delicate as she asked, "Do you have any enemies?"

Greta and Lisa looked at each other, surprised by the question. "What do you mean?" asked Lisa, wiping away tears.

Beth explained, "I mean, have you ever received any threats or experienced any hostility because you're a gay couple with a daughter?"

Greta shook her head. "No, we've never had any issues like that."

Lisa added, "We've always felt accepted and supported by our community."

Beth nodded, making a note in her notepad. She had to explore every possibility, but it seemed unlikely that the couple's sexuality played a role in Christa's disappearance. "Can you tell me more about Christa?"

The couple's faces lit up as they began to talk about their daughter. They showed Beth pictures of her and told her about her hobbies and interests.

"She loves to read," said Lisa, showing Beth a picture of Christa holding a book. "She's always got her nose buried in one."

"And she's a really good student," said Greta. "She's in the gifted program at school."

Beth listened intently, trying to get a sense of Christa's personality and habits. As the couple continued to talk, Beth was nearly overwhelmed with sadness. She wondered what kind of person would take a child away from her family, from the people who loved her most.

"Do you mind if I keep this?" asked Beth, holding up the picture of Christa.

Lisa smiled sadly. "Of course, you can have it. We have a few copies printed out for law enforcement already."

Beth thanked her and tucked the photo into her notepad. "I'm going to need to see Christa's room and talk to anyone who might have seen her yesterday," said Beth, standing up.

Greta and Lisa nodded and led her down the hall to Christa's room. The walls were adorned with posters of books and a whiteboard with math equations scrawled across it. Beth took a moment to look around, taking in the details of the room. She noticed a book on the nightstand, and she picked it up, flipping through the pages.

"This is one of her favorites," said Lisa, coming up behind her. "She's read it three times already."

Beth made a mental note to keep an eye out for the book in case it held any clues, though it seemed unlikely. She looked around the rest of the room, taking note of any other items that might be useful.

"Can you think of anyone who might have seen her yesterday afternoon?" asked Beth, turning back to the couple.

Greta shook her head. "We've talked to all her friends, and no one's seen her since she left school."

Lisa added, "She usually comes straight home, but sometimes she stops at the library on the way. We checked there, but they haven't seen her either."

Beth nodded, making notes in her notepad. "I have another delicate question... about Christa's donor?"

Greta and Lisa looked at each other, clearly surprised by the question. "What do you mean?" asked Greta.

"I mean, do you know anything about Christa's biological father? Has anyone ever tried to contact her or you about him?"

Greta shook her head. "No, we used a sperm bank, and we don't know anything about the donor."

Lisa said, "And we've never heard anything from anyone claiming to be her biological father. We've always been her parents, as far as we're concerned."

She nodded, making a note in her notepad. She had to explore every possibility, but it seemed unlikely Christa's biological father played a role in her disappearance.

As Beth left Christa's room, she couldn't help but feel a sense of urgency. The longer a child was missing, the less likely they were to be found. From what she remembered from training, about seventy-five percent of abducted children were dead within three hours, and almost ninety percent were dead within a day. She had to work quickly if she wanted to have any chance of finding Christa alive. She made her way back to the living room, where Greta and Lisa were waiting for her.

"I'm going to need a list of anyone who might have had contact with Christa recently," said Beth, pulling out her notepad.

Greta and Lisa exchanged a worried glance before Greta spoke up. "She doesn't have a lot of friends, and we're not really in contact with anyone else, but we can give you a list of her teachers and the parents of the few friends she has."

Beth nodded, jotting down notes. She needed to talk to anyone who might have seen Christa or knew something about her whereabouts.

"Thank you. I'll start there. I'll be in touch if I need anything else."

Greta and Lisa thanked her, and Beth made her way out of the house, with Grimm following closely behind. She couldn't shake the feeling of urgency as she got back into the RV and started it up. Time was running out if she wanted to find Christa alive.

Chapter Two

IT WAS IMPORTANT TO work with local law enforcement on the case, so she decided to head to the Olympia Police Department to introduce herself and offer her assistance. She'd just omit her lapse in protocol from visiting the parents first.

She parked the RV in the parking lot and walked inside, her badge and notepad in hand. Grimm trotted politely alongside her, his nose quivering at all the new stimuli.

As she approached the front desk, a uniformed officer greeted her. "May I help you?" he asked.

"Yes, I'm Detective Beth Danville from Denver. I'm here to offer my assistance with the Christa Stevens case," said Beth, showing him her badge.

The officer looked at her skeptically. "I'm sorry, but we already have everything under control. We don't need any outside help."

Beth persisted. "I understand, but I think it would be beneficial to work together. I have a lot of experience with missing child cases and could provide valuable insight."

The officer sighed. "Look, I appreciate the offer, but we have protocols to follow. You're not a part of our department, and we have everything under control."

Beth's frustration was building, but she remained calm. "I understand that, but I'm here to help in any way I can. A detective from Denver, Cassia Moringa, should have called ahead to vouch for me?"

Just then, a woman's voice called out from down the hall, "Officer Johnson, let her in. I've been expecting her."

The officer looked relieved and stepped aside to let Beth and Grimm through. She followed the voice down the hallway and into an office.

The woman behind the desk introduced herself as Detective Angela Rodriguez, the lead investigator on the case. She shook Beth's hand and thanked her for coming.

"I appreciate your willingness to help, Detective Danville and Grimm," said Detective Rodriguez, smiling briefly at the dog, "But I have to warn you, we have protocols in place for working with outside agencies. You're welcome to assist us, but you need to follow our procedures."

Beth nodded, understanding the situation. "Of course. We just want to help."

Detective Rodriguez appeared to appreciate Beth's eagerness as she explained their procedures to her before adding, "We've been working around the clock on this case since we began investigating yesterday afternoon. It's been all over the news, and we have a lot of resources dedicated to it. We've already conducted interviews with family and friends, checked surveillance footage, and searched local areas."

Beth nodded, impressed with their thoroughness. "That's great, Detective Rodriguez. Is there anything else I can do to help?"

Detective Rodriguez thought for a moment before speaking. "Actually, your dog could be helpful. Detective Moringa told me about your work with scent detection, and it could be useful in locating Christa."

Beth smiled, knowing Grimm's skills could be an asset. "Absolutely. Grimm is trained in scent work, and he's helped recover missing children before. Last year, he played a crucial role in the recovery of a kidnapped daughter of a Colorado state senator." A few months before Beth's own life derailed, but she pushed aside the thought as it came to her.

Detective Rodriguez looked impressed. "That's quite a feat. We could use his help in searching the areas we haven't been able to cover yet. I'll have one of our officers work with you to coordinate the search."

Beth nodded in agreement. "That sounds like a good plan. I'll work with your officer and see what we can find."

Detective Rodriguez nodded and handed Beth a folder with information on the case. "Here's what we have so far. We've been focusing on the area around Christa's school and her usual walking route home, but we haven't found any clues yet."

Beth thanked her and took the folder, scanning through the information. The police had already spoken with Christa's friends and teachers and checked surveillance footage from the area. They had also conducted a search of nearby parks and wooded areas but hadn't found anything.

"I'll review the information and see if there's anything else we can do," said Beth, tucking the folder under her arm.

Detective Rodriguez nodded. "Please keep me updated on anything you find. And remember, we have procedures in place for working with outside agencies."

Beth nodded in agreement, understanding the importance of following protocol. "I will, thank you."

She left the detective's office to wait in the entry. The officer finally arrived, and she introduced herself as Officer Lee. She handed Beth a map of the area they planned to search and explained the plan of action.

"I also brought Christa's teddy bear," said Officer Lee, holding up a small stuffed animal. "We thought Grimm could sniff it and get a better sense of her scent before we start the search."

Beth nodded and handed the bear to Grimm, who eagerly sniffed it. She could see the focus in his eyes as he picked up the scent. "Let's get started," she said, gesturing to the door.

They stepped out of the police department and into the bright sunshine. The air was crisp, and Beth could feel a light breeze on her skin. She looked around at the scenery, taking note of the buildings and the street layout. The area was mostly residential, with tree-lined streets and small houses with well-kept yards.

Officer Lee led the way, and Beth followed closely behind with Grimm by her side. He sniffed the air, his nose twitching as he picked up the scent of Christa's teddy bear.

They walked along the route that Christa usually took home from school, checking alleyways and side streets for any signs of the missing girl. Grimm led them down a narrow alley, his nose close to the ground as he followed the scent. Beth's her heart raced as they walked, hoping they would find a clue to lead them to Christa.

Suddenly, Grimm stopped in his tracks, his tail wagging excitedly. Beth followed his gaze and saw a small object lying on the ground. She rushed over and picked it up, examining it closely.

It was a hair clip, and she recognized it from one of the pictures in the folder Detective Rodriguez had given her. They might be on the right track.

"Good job, Grimm," she said, patting him on the head.

Officer Lee came over to inspect the hair clip. It was delicate and ornate, made of gold and silver with a small ruby at its center.

"I've seen this before," said Beth, her voice echoing in the alleyway as she opened the file to show the officer one of the photos Lisa and Greta had given the department.

"It looks the same to me," said Officer Lee. She paused for a moment to call for the Forensic Investigations Division to send out a unit. Once she'd taped off the area, she said, "They'll be here soon. We can keep going."

She nodded, and they resumed walking, following Grimm, who was still focused on the scent. As they walked, Beth noticed a small park at the end of the alley. There was a swing set and a slide, and she wondered if Christa had ever played there.

"Grimm, search," she said, pointing to the park.

Grimm eagerly bounded ahead, his nose close to the ground. Beth and Officer Lee followed, keeping a close eye on their surroundings.

As they approached the swing set, Beth noticed something on the ground. It was a piece of paper, and she picked it up, examining it closely.

It was a drawing of a cat, and she recognized Rudolph from the Stevens' home. "This is Christa's cat. I think it is anyway. If so, Christa must have drawn it. We need to get this to Detective Rodriguez," said Beth, tucking the drawing into her notepad.

Officer Lee nodded, and they continued their search. They scoured the park and surrounding areas, but they didn't find any other clues.

As the sun began to set, they decided to call it a day. She stopped by the station to drop off the drawing and the barrette with Detective Rodriguez. After that, she climbed back into the RV, her mind racing with thoughts of the case as she drove to the closest RV park. She hoped they were getting closer to finding Christa, but there was still a long road ahead.

THE NEXT MORNING, BETH woke early, still feeling the weight of the case on her shoulders. They had to make progress soon, or the chances of finding Christa alive would continue to decrease.

As she sat at the kitchen table, sipping coffee, her phone rang. It was a number she didn't recognize, but she answered it anyway. "Hello?"

"Beth? It's Patty Schumer," said a familiar voice on the other end.

"Patty? Wow, it's been a while," Beth was surprised to hear from her former academy classmate. Patty's career had been short, ended when she decided to beat up a pedophile. Beth understood her reasons but thought she'd flushed a chance to make a real difference by beating just one.

"Yeah, sorry to call out of the blue like this, but I saw the news about the missing girl in Olympia. I spoke with Detective Rodriguez last night, and she mentioned you. Small world. She told me your dog found a clue," said Patty.

Beth's ears perked up at the mention of Grimm. "Yes, he did. He found her hair clip, and there was also a picture of a cat that she probably drew."

"I hope it leads somewhere," said Patty. "Look, I know I'm not in the area, but I wanted to offer my help. I've been working undercover on my own dime to target human trafficking rings that focus on teenage prostitutes. I know it's not the same as this case, but I have some experience with these types of situations."

Beth paused, considering the offer. Patty's work sounded dangerous and controversial, but her heart was in the right place. "I appreciate the offer. Let me talk to Detective Rodriguez and see if we can work out something."

"Great, just let me know," said Patty before hanging up.

After hanging up with Patty, Beth was glad someone else was willing to help with the case. She had to convince Detective Rodriguez Patty could be a valuable asset though.

She quickly dialed the detective's number and explained the situation. "I know it sounds unconventional, but Patty has experience working with human trafficking rings. She's been working undercover to target them and could provide us with valuable insight."

Detective Rodriguez was hesitant at first, but Beth could sense her willingness to consider the offer. "I don't know, Detective Danville."

"Beth," she inserted, hoping to soften the detective.

"We have procedures in place for working with outside agencies, and we don't want to compromise the investigation."

"I understand that, but Patty's trustworthy. We went through the academy together, and I know she has the best intentions. She's just trying to make a difference...Angela," said Beth, hoping to persuade her and increase their sense of camaraderie by using first names.

Angela probably understood the tactic but finally relented. "Okay, have her come down here and meet with me, but she needs to follow our procedures and work with us, not on her own."

"I'll be sure to relay that." She couldn't help feeling it was a message, or at least a pointed reminder, to herself as well that she was involved in the case only due to the Olympia Police Department's goodwill.

A few minutes later, her phone rang again, and it was Patty. "Hey, Beth, did you talk to Detective Rodriguez?"

"Yeah, I did," Beth said, explaining the conversation she'd just had. "She said come to her if you're willing to follow her rules and work with her department."

"Of course, I understand. That's not a problem." After relaying her expected arrival time, she hung up.

As Beth hung up the phone, she realized she didn't know much about what Patty had been up to. She made a mental note to ask her when she arrived.

She turned to Grimm, who was lying on the couch. "All right, let's get to work," she said, grabbing her notepad and heading out the door.

Beth decided to retrace the previous officers' steps and start canvassing the neighborhood again with Grimm. He was like a secret weapon. She hoped.

At first, they found nothing until they stopped at a nearby convenience store close enough to the school to make it worth asking if anyone had seen her. She and Grimm walked in, freezing almost immediately.

"You can't bring your dog in," said the kid behind the counter.

She pointed to his vest. "He's a cop."

He looked skeptical. "Yeah? Where's his badge?"

She pointed to it on the vest and flashed her own, hopefully quickly enough he didn't see it was issued from Colorado. "We're working the missing child case. Have you seen her?"

The young man frowned as she showed him Christa's picture. "Oh, yeah, I remember her. She's a regular customer. She came in around three-thirty yesterday and bought some chips and a soda."

Beth made a note in her notepad. "Did she say anything to you? Did she seem upset or scared?"

The clerk thought for a moment. "No, she seemed pretty happy. She chatted with me for a bit before she left."

Beth thanked the clerk and moved on to the next location, a small park where Christa was known to go after school. She showed a picture of Christa to a group of teenagers hanging out on the swings.

One of them nodded. "Yeah, I remember her. She was here yesterday, playing with her cat."

Beth's heart skipped a beat at the mention of the cat. "What do you mean, her cat?"

The teenager shrugged. "She had a cat with her. It was really cute."

Did that mean Christa had gone home and then ventured out again? "Do you remember anything about the cat?"

One of the girls spoke up. "It was a thin black kitten with matted fur. Christa was trying to take care of it."

Beth nodded, jotting down the description. That definitely didn't match the chubby tabby she'd seen at the Stevens' home. "Did anyone else see the cat or know where it came from?"

The teenagers shrugged, and one of them said, "We thought it was a stray. Christa said she was trying to find its home."

Beth started to thank them, but her phone rang, interrupting their conversation. It was Angela. It was too soon for Patty to have arrived, so the call had to be about something else. Her stomach curled with dread as she imagined the horrible things they might have discovered. *Please let it be a break.* "This is Danville."

"We've got a lead on Christa," said Angela. "We found her backpack in a dumpster behind a convenience store. We're heading over there now."

Beth's heart raced as she hung up the phone after getting the address. It was the same store they'd been in a short time ago, so she and Grimm headed back that way at a jog.

She wouldn't have stopped, but Grimm's ears perked, and she heard a tiny, "Meow," at the same time he woofed softly. She bent closer, pushing aside a section of bush, and saw a thin black kitten. It was with two other littermates, and she assumed it was the cat Christa had found. If the cat was back here, either Christa had realized it had a family, albeit it was still homeless, or someone had snatched her before she had a chance to try to find its home.

Grimm was interested in the kittens, but they had more pressing matters. "Search," she said, and he took off like a shot, heading back toward the convenience store.

There were several police cars already parked outside when Beth arrived at the convenience store. Beth's heart was pounding in her chest when she and Grimm walked toward Angela as she gestured them to follow her around the back of the building, where the dumpster was located.

While walking with Angela, Beth told her about the kitten. The other detective mulled it over. "I'd bet that helps us pinpoint when she was taken. Surely before four p.m. since she was in the convenience store around three-thirty. She must have found the kitten, approached that group, and then someone snatched her, and she left the kitten behind."

"That makes sense to me too." It was purely speculation, but a lot of their job involved educated guesswork.

As they approached the dumpster, there was a crowd of officers gathered around the dumpster. Angela held up a hand to stop Beth as they got closer.

"Stay back, Detective. We need to process the scene," said she, gesturing to the Forensic Investigations Division officers, who were collecting evidence.

Beth nodded, understanding the need to be careful. She watched as the officers carefully removed the backpack from the dumpster and placed it in a plastic bag for further examination.

As they finished, Angela turned to Beth. "We'll need to talk to the store owner and anyone who might have seen something."

"Yes, let's talk to the store owner," said Beth, her mind already working on the possibilities.

They made their way inside the store, where the owner was nervously pacing behind the counter. The kid who'd spoken to Beth earlier was watching them curiously but busy checking out customers.

"Can I help you, officers?" he asked, eyeing them warily.

"We're investigating the disappearance of Christa Stevens," said Angela. "We found her backpack in your dumpster. Do you know anything about it?"

The owner's eyes widened in shock. "No, I had no idea. I saw the police cars outside and thought it was a routine traffic stop or something."

Beth stepped forward, trying to put the man at ease. "Can you tell us if you saw anything unusual yesterday afternoon? Did you see Christa or anyone else who looked suspicious?"

The store owner thought for a moment before speaking. "Now that you mention it, I did see a man hanging around outside the store for a while. He was wearing a hoodie, and I couldn't see his face. He was acting strange, looking around like he was...ready to pounce. I don't know how else to describe it.."

Beth's heart sank at the mention of a suspicious man. "Do you think you could describe him to a sketch artist?"

The owner nodded. "Yeah, I'll do whatever I can to help, but his face was almost entirely covered by the hoodie. That seems really suspicious now that I think about it."

As they finished talking to the store owner, Beth's phone rang again. This time, it was Patty.

"Beth, I'm here. Where do you need me?"

"We're at a convenience store on 4th and Main. Meet us here, and we'll fill you in."

Chapter Three

AS BETH AND ANGELA waited for Patty to arrive, they watched as officers continued to sift through the contents of the dumpster. Grimm was on high alert, his nose twitching as he scanned the area.

Suddenly, he started pawing at a napkin that had been tossed aside from the dumpster. Beth leaned in closer, trying to catch a whiff of what had caught Grimm's attention.

"What is it, boy?" she asked, and Grimm let out a low growl as he pawed at the napkin again.

Angela approached them, looking concerned. "What's going on?"

Beth pointed to the napkin. "Grimm picked up a scent on this. It could be a clue."

The detective nodded and called over one of the evidence technicians. "Bag that napkin and send it to the lab for analysis. We need to know if there's anything on it that could help us."

As they waited for the evidence technician to take away the napkin, Patty arrived, looking serious and focused.

After brief introductions, she got straight to business. "I've got some intel on a guy named Lenny Mendez. He's been trying to hook up with young girls online, and I've been posing as a decoy to draw him out."

Angela raised an eyebrow. "And you're doing this on your own? That's dangerous."

Patty shrugged. "I know what I'm doing. I've got him on the hook, and I think I can force him to give us some information."

Beth nodded, impressed by Patty's bravery and resourcefulness. "That could be a big break for us. Let's go talk to Angela and see if we can coordinate with her."

As they made their way over to Angela, Grimm suddenly started pulling at his leash, tugging Beth toward a nearby alleyway.

"What is it, boy?" she asked, following Grimm's lead.

He led her to a rusty metal door at the back of the alleyway. It was covered in peeling paint and looked like it hadn't been opened in years.

A knot formed in her stomach. "I think we need to check this out," she said, drawing her gun and nodding to Angela and Patty.

Angela also drew her gun as they approached the door. Patty took a taser from her purse, ignoring Angela's look of dismay.

As they got closer, they heard muffled voices and the sound of machinery coming from inside.

Beth signaled for Grimm to sniff around the door, and he immediately started whining and pawing at the metal. "There's something in there. We need to be careful."

She gave the door a hard shove, and it creaked open with a loud screech. Inside, they found a small room filled with industrial equipment and machinery. But what really caught her attention was a series of photographs scattered on a nearby table. The pictures showed young girls, some of them no more than thirteen, dressed in provocative clothing and posing for the camera. There was photography equipment, but the voices they'd heard were gone. "Whoever was here must have scattered," said Beth, sickened as she looked away from the pictures while Angela donned gloves to collect them.

Angela nodded, pulling out her radio. "This is Detective Rodriguez. We have suspects fleeing the building. We need backup at the front entrance."

Beth took a deep breath, trying to calm her racing heart. They had to be careful, but they also had to act fast if they were going to find any evidence that could lead them to Christa. She made her way back through the room with the photographs, looking for anything that could help them. Grimm beside her was a comforting presence.

As she searched, she noticed a stack of papers sitting on the corner of the table. She picked them up, scanning the contents. They were orders for various types of equipment, including cameras, lights, and computers. One of the orders caught her eye—it was for a video camera with a unique serial number.

She quickly jotted down the number in her notepad, knowing it could be a vital piece of evidence. They could use it to trace the camera back to its owner and hopefully find out who was behind this operation.

As she looked around, she noticed a door at the back of the room. She gestured to Angela and Patty to follow her as she made her way toward it.

As they opened the door, they found themselves in a small hallway with another door at the end. Beth heard footsteps echoing through the hallway. "They must have gone this way."

Angela nodded, pulling out her radio. "This is Detective Rodriguez. We need backup at the back entrance too."

Officers responded over the radio as Beth pushed open the door at the end of the hallway. They found themselves in a large open room, filled with more industrial equipment and machinery. There were several doors leading off the room, and they odd rustling noises coming from one of them.

Beth gestured to Grimm to stay close as they cautiously approached the door. Her heart pounded as she readied her gun.

As they burst through the door, they found themselves in a dimly lit corridor, with more doors leading off it.

"It's like a maze that never ends," said Patty, sounding grumpy.

Beth nodded. "We need to thoroughly search this place. Let's split up and see what we can find."

They split up and began to search the various rooms and corridors of the building. She was glad to have Grimm with her, but her nerves were still strung taut as she opened one door after another, not knowing what she might find.

In one room, she found a desk covered in papers and notebooks. As she flipped through them, she realized that they were ledgers documenting the trafficking and exploitation of young girls. The ledger didn't include their names. Just "cute" monikers like Sweet/Tight. It was nauseating. After bagging it, she slid it in her purse and moved on.

In another room, she found a closet filled with racks of sexy clothes in sizes that had no right to exist and several vanities spread with makeup. It was clear girls had been here, and Beth's stomach turned at the thought of what they must have gone through.

Suddenly, she heard footsteps getting closer, and a figure appeared from one of the doors, running toward her and Grimm. It was a man, and he was holding a metal pipe. She didn't hesitate. She raised her gun and fired, hitting the perp in the shoulder. He stumbled and fell to the ground, dropping the pipe.

Angela and Patty came running, quickly restraining him as Beth approached to loom over him. The man was writhing in pain, and the bullet had gone clean through his shoulder. Angela called for an ambulance as she and Patty handcuffed him.

While they waited for the ambulance to arrive, Beth looked around the room. It was set up like a studio, with lights and cameras pointed at a bed in the center of the room.

She approached the bed, feeling sickened by what she saw. The sheets were stained and rumpled, and there were handcuffs and restraints scattered around the room. It was clear what kind of operation was being run here, and it made her blood boil.

As the ambulance arrived, they loaded the injured suspect into the back and drove to the hospital. They returned to the building to help secure the scene and gather evidence. The rest of their search turned up nothing, and Angela said, "Forensic techs are ready to come in, so we need to clear out."

"Understood. Come, Grimm." He bounded back to her, and she walked out with Angela and Patty. As they made their way back to the front entrance, uniformed officers escorted several more suspects out of the building in handcuffs. She couldn't help but feel a sense of satisfaction as she realized they had just taken down a major operation involved in child trafficking and exploitation.

As they made their way out of the warehouse, Beth's mind was racing with the possibilities of what they might find next. They had made a major breakthrough in taking down the trafficking ring, but Christa was still missing.

They walked back to the convenience store, where officers were still sifting through the contents of the dumpster. Grimm was eager to get to work and started pawing at a nearby pizza box.

Beth watched him closely as he sniffed around the box. She noticed a strange look on his face, as if he had picked up on something important.

"What is it, boy?" she asked, kneeling beside him.

Grimm let out a low growl as he pawed at the pizza box. Beth took a closer look and noticed a small piece of paper stuck to the bottom of the box.

After accepting gloves from Angela, she carefully removed the paper and examined it. It was a torn piece of a flyer for a local youth center, with the address and phone number partially visible. "We need to follow up on this," she said to Angela and Patty, who nodded in agreement.

They made their way back to their vehicles and headed toward the youth center. As they arrived, a group of teenagers gathered outside, chatting and laughing, stopped to stare at them.

When they drew nearer, she saw an older man standing with them. He seemed to be part of their chatter, but he stood out like a sore thumb.

Beth caught her breath when she looked at the man's name tag. "Lenny," she whispered to herself. She couldn't help but wonder if this was the same Lenny Patty had been trying to entice online.

Before she could say anything, Patty leaned in and whispered to both her and Angela, "That's him. I recognize him from his picture."

As if on cue, Grimm's nose started twitching, and he let out a low growl as he caught the scent of the man. Beth could see the hairs on the back of his neck standing on end as he pushed Lenny into a corner.

"What's going on? Call off your dog, lady," said Lenny in an irritatingly high-pitched voice.

Beth, Angela, and Patty quickly surrounded him, making it clear he wasn't going anywhere. Patty stepped forward, her eyes blazing with anger. "Do you know who I am?" she asked, holding up her phone to show Lenny a picture of herself. "I'm Pattycakes14. The girl you've been talking to online."

Lenny's face went pale as he realized he'd been caught. Beth and Angela stepped forward, flanking Patty as they cornered Lenny.

"We know about the trafficking ring," said Beth, her voice firm. "And we know you're involved." It was a hunch, but she injected confidence in her tone when she said, "We know you're using this place to recruit girls."

Lenny's eyes darted around the entrance and street, looking for a way out, but there was nowhere to go. Grimm was still growling at him, and the three detectives had him surrounded.

"What do you want?" he finally spat out, his voice shaky.

"We want to know everything you know," said Angela, her voice cold and hard. "And we want you to help us find the missing girl."

Lenny's face went even paler at the mention of the missing girl. "I don't know anything," he stammered.

Beth leaned in close, her voice low and threatening. "Don't lie to us, Lenny. We know about the production studio. We know about the girls. And we know you're involved. If you don't start talking, we're going to make sure everyone knows what you've been up to."

Lenny looked at the teens nearby, who were watching avidly, desperation written all over his face. Finally, he nodded. "Okay, okay. I'll tell you what I know. Let's go somewhere private first."

They escorted Lenny to an empty room in the youth center and sat him down at a table. Patty pulled out her phone and started recording, making it clear they had evidence of everything he said. "I can do this because I'm not a cop," she said in a chatty tone to Lenny. "Smile for YouTube, you perv."

He started sweating and shaking. "Don't do this. I'll be ruined. My wife will leave me."

"She deserves to know how disgusting you are, but if you cooperate, the video disappears." Patty snapped her fingers but didn't put down the phone.

When his pleading expression failed to move Beth or Angela, he lowered his head. "What do you want to know?"

As they questioned him, Lenny's fear turned to anger. "I didn't do anything wrong. I was just trying to make some extra money. I never touched the girls. I was just supposed to lure them in. That goes for you too, Pattycake," he said with a spiteful twist of his lips. "I never wanted you."

"Just the girl I pretended to be. I'm heartbroken."

Beth's blood boiled as she listened to him try to justify his actions. She had heard it all before, and there was no excuse for what he had done.

But they pressed on, asking him about the trafficking ring and the missing girl. When they mentioned the production studio, Lenny's face went pale. "I didn't know anything about that," he said, his voice trembling. "I just did what I was told. I brought in the girls but never did any of the hands-on stuff."

Beth leaned in close, her voice low and menacing. "Who told you what to do, Lenny? Who's in charge of all this?"

Lenny hesitated, looking around the room as if he was trying to think of a way out. Finally, he spoke. "There's a guy named Hector. He's the one who runs the whole thing."

Beth felt a thrill of excitement run through her. They finally had a name. She leaned in closer, her eyes locked on Lenny's. "Where can we find him?"

Lenny shook his head. "I don't know. He's always moving around, but I can give you a phone number. He'll call me back in a few days to give me my next assignment."

Beth tore off a page from her notebook. "Write down the number." She hated to let his grimy hands touch her pen, but she wanted that information, so she handed it over.

He wrote it down and pushed it back to her. Beth left the pen on the table and put the paper in her pocket.

"We're square now, right?"

"I have a question," said Beth.

Lenny was sweating profusely. "Yeah, what's that?"

"Why did your people take Christa? You seem to be going for an older crowd."

He nodded. "That's right. We go for girls who are fourteen or older, who know what they're agreeing to do. We don't snatch kids. I don't know nothing about this Christa. Just what I seen on the news."

He sounded so sanctimonious, like tricking teenagers into dirty movies was so much better than kidnapping a child. She grunted in disgust as Grimm growled at him, clearly picking up on her mood.

"Can I go now?" asked Lenny, sweating heavier.

"Yep. Straight to jail," said Angela as she extracted handcuffs.

He tried to bolt. Of course, he did. Idiot. It didn't take much for the three of them to subdue him. All Grimm had to do was growl at Lenny, and he collapsed backward against the table. As Angela handcuffed Lenny, he protested and demanded to know what was going on. "You said you weren't going to arrest me," he shouted.

Angela ignored him, instead calling for a police car to take him to the station for questioning. Beth could see the fear in Lenny's eyes as he was led away, and she was thrilled he wouldn't be preying on more young girls.

"We need to tell them what's going on," said Angela, gesturing to a woman standing in the hallway. She looked frantic with worry.

"Yeah." Beth followed Angela and Patty, with Grimm at her six.

The woman hurried toward them, and her nametag identified her as Director Phillips. "What's going on here?" She sounded somewhere between frightened and annoyed.

"You've had a pervert volunteering here, Director Phillips," said Patty with no tact. "He's been recruiting young girls."

The woman gasped, her red hair suddenly a bright contrast to her now-alabaster complexion. "No. He passed a background screening."

"A surprising number of pervs can," said Patty.

The director's face paled to almost bloodless as Beth and Patty filled her in on the details. "We need you to make sure he's not allowed back here," Beth said firmly, her voice leaving no room for negotiation as she ended the explanation.

The director nodded, clearly shaken. "Of course. I'll make sure that all the staff are aware of the situation."

"And tighten up your screening protocols," said Patty with a glare.

"Of course." The director seemed on the verge of fainting and collapsed against the wall as they turned away from her.

Cautiously, Beth and Patty stepped out of the community center. A group of teenage girls were loitering outside, their eyes glued to the two police officers. Beth marched up to them, introducing herself and asking if they knew anything about Lenny's disappearance or any suspicious activity that may have occurred recently.

The girls all shook their heads, but there was one among them who seemed particularly uncomfortable. Her face had gone pale, and she wouldn't make eye contact with anyone. Beth motioned for Patty to follow her as she and Grimm followed the girl, whose bejeweled backpack said her name was Shana. She was , determined to get some answers. As they cornered Shana in around the block, Beth saw fear in her eyes.

"What do you want?" she asked, her voice barely above a whisper.

"We just want to ask you a few questions," said Beth, trying to keep her tone gentle. "Do you know anything about Lenny or any suspicious activity going on in the area?"

Shana shook her head, but Beth could tell she was lying. Guilt was written all over the girl's face.

"Please, Shana," said Patty, her voice firm. "We're trying to stop something really bad from happening. We need your help."

Shana looked around nervously before finally whispering, "I...I made some movies for Lenny's people."

Beth's heart sank as she realized what Shana was saying. "What kind of movies?" she asked, dreading the answer.

"For money," Shana said, tears starting to form in her eyes. "They said it was just for fun, but now I don't know."

Beth placed a hand on the girl's shoulder, trying to comfort her. "It's going to be okay," she said, looking at Patty. "Let's get her to the station and see if we can find out more."

Chapter Four

IT TOOK A COUPLE OF hours for Shana to talk to them. Angela had called her mother to get permission to speak with the girl, and she returned to Beth and Patty watching Shana fidget through the window of the interrogation room. "Her mother gave permission. Total waste of space. I'm sure she was high and has no idea I even called by now."

Beth grimaced as Patty said, "A lot of girls like Shana end up in this situation because they're forced to grow up too quickly or think easy money is the way out of their problems."

"I hate making her feel like a criminal, but maybe she's been sweating long enough to tell us everything." Angela looked regretful as she took the lead.

Beth and Grimm followed behind with Patty bringing up the rear.

Shana grimaced at the sight of them. Her eyes were red, and she was clearly holding back tears.

"We aren't going to hurt you," said Angela.

"You aren't in trouble," said Beth. "We just need to know everything."

It seemed to be Grimm who got through to her. He approached with a low whine, wagging his tail, and put his head on her lap. After a moment, Shana started petting him. She visibly relaxed the more she interacted with the Belgian Malinois.

Finally, she spoke. " I'll tell you what I know, but you can't tell anyone else. They'll hurt me if they find out."

Beth and Patty nodded, encouraging her to continue, as Angela said, "I guarantee no one is going to hurt you, honey."

"So does Grimm," said Beth.

Shana managed a shaky smile as she petted his furry head. "Is that your name? Grimm?" When he wagged his tail and licked her hand, she giggled, sounding much younger than fourteen or fifteen for a moment.

Holding onto Grimm seemed to give her the courage to speak. "I've been making movies for some guys," Shana said, her voice shaking. "They paid me good money, but I didn't know what it was for to start with. Then, after I arrived, they sort of convinced and sort of forced me to make the first one. When I tried to stop, they told me they'd show the movie to everyone in my life if I didn't keep working for them." She sniffled. "The one in charge told me it didn't matter, since I wasn't a virgin anymore. I'd gotten the hard part out of the way."

Beth and Patty exchanged a look. It was clear what kind of movies Shana was talking about. Rage swelled in Beth, but she struggled to keep her voice soft. "Who were these guys?"

"I don't know their names," Shana said, "But they had a studio near the convenience store. That's where I went to make the movies."

Beth's heart skipped a beat. That was the same building where they had found the photos of the young girls, along with the makeshift studio and bed.

"What about Christa?" asked Patty. "Did you see her there?"

Beth held out the photo of Christa she'd been carrying in her pocket.

After examining the smiling brunette waif in the photo, Shana shook her head. "No, I've never seen her before."

Beth's stomach pitted when she realized this group might not have Christa.

"What do these guys look like?" asked Beth, hoping to get some identifying information.

"They were white, in their thirties or forties, and they always wore sunglasses," said Shana, her voice trembling. "I've only ever seen them from behind. They always tied me up and blindfolded me before..." She broke into a sob, bending forward to hug Grimm. He cuddled closer, nudging her cheek with his nose as he looked at Beth.

She mouthed, "Good boy," letting the dog soothe the girl in a way none of them could. She wished the girl had better information. It wasn't much to go on, but it was better than nothing.

"What about the girls you saw at the studio?" Patty asked. "Did you recognize any of them?"

Shana hesitated before speaking. "Most of them were around my age, fourteen to sixteen. I didn't recognize any of them, but some of them looked scared. Like they didn't want to be there."

Beth's heart sank. Christa didn't fit the profile of the pornography ring's usual victim. "Thank you, Shana," said Beth, patting her on the shoulder. "You've been a big help."

Shana nodded, still crying softly. She seemed to want to cling to Grimm, and Beth would have let her, but Chief Reyes stuck his head in and said, "Angela, hallway."

Beth and Patty stayed with Shana, who seemed content to pet Grimm for the rest of his life. He didn't seem to mind either. His eyes were closed, and he was clearly enjoying the attention.

They snapped open when Angela returned, and his posture changed. It was like he sensed something in her mood. He gave Shana one last nudge with his nose before moving to stand beside Beth, his posture at attention.

"Hey, what's up?" asked Beth.

"We just got a call about another missing girl." Angela's dark eyes reflected anger and worry.

Beth's heart sank. "Where was she last seen?"

"At a park on the other side of town. We're heading over there now."

"What about her?" asked Patty, nodding toward Shana.

"Social Services is sending over someone to talk to her. It's in their hands now."

Beth felt awful for the girl and only hoped her life wouldn't be too disrupted by everything that had occurred.

Moments later, they rushed to Angela's car and drove to the park, with Patty following behind in her vehicle. As they arrived, uniformed officers canvassed the area, questioning anyone who might have seen the missing girl. Angela hurried out of the car.

It took Beth a moment longer to get Grimm, and then she followed Angela, who was speaking with one of the officers.

"What do we know?" asked Beth, her voice low.

"She's nine years old and named Emily," said Angela, her brow furrowed. "Last seen at the playground by her house. No witnesses so far."

Beth took a deep breath, trying to stay calm. They had to find Emily, but they also couldn't lose sight of their search for Christa.

"We need to split up and start looking for any clues," Beth said, gesturing for Grimm to join her. "Is there anything of hers he can smell?"

"Not yet," said Angela as she and Patty walked the opposite direction to look for clues.

As they began to search the park, Beth was overwhelmed with dread. The thought of another missing girl was almost too much to bear. She should be able to handle it professionally, but this case felt far too personal. She had to push those feelings aside and focus on finding any evidence that could lead them to Emily and hopefully, Christa.

Hours passed as they searched the park, but they found nothing. As night began to fall, they regrouped with Angela and the other officers.

"We're not getting anywhere," said Angela, frustration lacing her voice. "We need to keep looking, but we also need to start thinking about bringing in more resources."

"What do you mean?" asked Beth.

"I'll see if I can convince the chief to call in the FBI, and in the meantime, we should all take a break." Angela rolled her shoulders, looking exhausted. "Anyone want to grab food?"

"I'm hungry," said Patty.

They looked at Beth expectantly, but she shook her head. "I just want sleep." If only it were so easy. Sleep had proven elusive these past few months.

She accepted a ride with Patty back to her RV and waved to her before she and Grimm entered. She served Grimm and considered eating too, but her stomach turned at the thought of food.

While he chowed down, she sat at the dinette. The silence around her only added to the weight of her thoughts. She poured herself a glass of whiskey from the bottle conveniently located in the locking cabinet above her head, hoping it would help quiet the storm brewing inside of her. But with each sip, she only felt more lost and alone.

The case had taken a toll on her, and the stress of it all had started to catch up with her. It was all too much to handle: The thought of never having a child with Joel, the memory of his death from pancreatic cancer just four months ago, and the endless search for Christa. She had always imagined her life with Joel, growing old together and raising a family. But now, all she had was an empty RV and an amazing dog for company.

As the tears began to flow down her cheeks, she couldn't help but wonder if it was all worth it. Why did she bother to keep going, day after day, in a world that was so cruel and unforgiving? She screamed in frustration, the sound muffled by the walls of her RV.

And then, she felt a soft nudge at her side. It was Grimm, her faithful companion, looking up at her with his deep brown eyes. In that moment, she realized she still had him to live for. She reached down to pet him, feeling his warmth and love radiating through her. He had been there for her through it all, never judging or leaving her side. As she looked into his eyes, she knew that she couldn't give up. Not yet, at least.

She wiped away her tears and took a deep breath, resolve washing over her. She had to keep going, to keep fighting for justice for Christa and for all the other girls caught up in this terrible world of exploitation and trafficking.

With a sense of purpose, she poured herself another whiskey and took a sip, feeling the liquid burn down her throat. She had to stay focused, but for now, the whiskey would have to do. It was one way to fall asleep, and she needed rest to tackle the investigation with a fresh mind tomorrow.

THE NEXT MORNING, BETH woke up to the sound of her phone ringing. She groggily reached for it, still feeling the effects of the whiskey from the night before. It was Angela, and she sounded urgent.

"Beth, we just got a call from the FBI. They're sending a team down to help us with the case. They should be here by this afternoon."

Beth sat up, suddenly feeling more alert. This was a major breakthrough, and it meant that they might finally have the resources they needed to find Christa.

"That's great news," she said, trying to sound upbeat. "I'll be there as soon as I can."

After a quick shower and a cup of coffee, Beth headed to the station. Excitement was building inside of her, knowing they were one step closer to finding the girls and bringing them home.

As she entered the briefing room, she saw the team of FBI agents already gathered around a table, studying a map of the area. Angela introduced her to the team leader, a no-nonsense woman named Agent Johnson.

"Agent Johnson, this is Detective Beth Danville. She and Grimm have been assisting the investigation," said Angela, making the introductions.

Beth shook Agent Johnson's hand, feeling a surge of adrenaline as she did so. This was it. They were finally going to crack the case.

"Good to meet you, Detective," Agent Johnson said, her voice cool and professional, though her gaze reflect a subtle hint of disdain, as if she'd already judged them as incompetent local rubes. "We've been briefed on the situation, and we appreciate your assistance when we request it."

"You're here to assist us," said Angela with a frown.

Agent Johnson arched a brow. "Are you new to how this works, Detective?"

Chief Reyes appeared then. "We all want the same thing," he said in a soothing tone as he nudged Angela toward a conference table. Beth followed, feeling uneasy about the FBI team. Just moments before, she'd been so optimistic, but now, it seemed like they weren't the type to work together.

"Let's get to work," she said, taking a seat at the table.

For the next several hours, they poured over the evidence they had gathered so far, discussing possible leads and strategies for finding Christa and Emily. It seemed every local suggestion had a flaw, and the FBI team was soon taking over. The Olympia PD was still in the room, but it was obvious they weren't part of the FBI's investigation.

As the day wore on, and the discussions grew more intense, Beth's thoughts started to drift. She couldn't help thinking about Joel and the life they had planned together. She had always been focused on her career, putting off starting a family in favor of chasing the next case or goal. And now, with Joel gone, she felt the weight of that decision more than ever.

Her thoughts were interrupted by Agent Johnson, who had noticed her distraction.

"Is everything okay, Detective?" she asked, her voice sharp.

Beth took a deep breath, trying to compose herself. "I'm fine. Just a little tired, that's all."

Agent Johnson sniffed. "We need everyone focused on this case, Detective. If you're not up to it, I suggest you take a break."

Beth felt a twinge of anger, but Agent Johnson was right. She couldn't afford to let her personal feelings get in the way of the investigation. She nodded, standing up from the table.

"I'll be back in an hour," she said, heading toward the door.

As she made her way outside, the reality of the situation hit her like a ton of bricks. They were no closer to finding Christa than they had been before, and the weight of that failure was crushing. She couldn't help but wonder if she had made the wrong choices in life, putting her career above all else.

She walked aimlessly through the streets of the town, lost in her thoughts. It was then that she saw a familiar face in the distance. It was Joel, walking toward her with a smile on his face. Beth's heart skipped a beat, and she started running toward him. But as she got closer, the figure started to fade, until all that was left was the memory of her husband.

She fell to her knees, tears streaming down her face. "Why did you have to leave me, Joel?" she cried out, her voice choked with emotion.

Grimm came up to her, nudging her with his nose, trying to comfort her. She hugged him tightly, feeling his warmth and love.

"I don't know how to do this without him," she whispered to him, feeling a sense of hopelessness wash over her. Yet as she looked into Grimm's eyes, she saw the love and loyalty there. He was her constant rock, and he would never leave her side.

Beth took a deep breath, attaining renewed clarity. She couldn't change the past, but she could control her future. That meant continuing the search for Christa and Emily, no matter how hard it was.

She stood up, wiping away her tears, and started walking back toward the station. She didn't know what the future held, but she knew that she had to keep going. For Joel, for herself, and for all the girls caught up in this terrible world.

As she entered the station, she heard the murmur of voices coming from the briefing room. She took a deep breath and walked in, determined to put her personal feelings aside and focus on the case.

Agent Johnson looked up as she entered, nodding in acknowledgement. "Glad you could join us, Detective," she said, her voice snarky.

Beth took a seat at the table, trying to shake off the weight of her emotions. She listened as the team discussed possible leads and strategies, feeling a renewed sense of determination.

As the meeting drew to a close, Agent Johnson turned to their table. "We'll be in touch with our next steps, Detectives. Don't do anything without our instructions."

Beth tensed, and so did Angela. Chief Reyes nodded. "Of course." He kept a pleasant smile until the FBI unit exited the conference room. Then his mask slipped. "Insufferable bunch of know-it-alls. That's why I didn't want to call them in, Ang."

Angela sighed. "I'm sorry. I thought they'd care more about helping than some professional rivalry."

The chief snorted. "They're obsessed with their pissing contest. Officially, we have to defer, since we invited them in, but..."

"Unofficially?" asked Beth with a small smile.

"I'm a lot more concerned about finding those girls than stepping on Feds' toes. Do what you've been doing." He nodded to them and winked. "We never had this talk, but I'll back you if needed." With that, he sauntered out of the room.

As they left the station a few minutes later, Angela turned to her. "You okay, Beth? You seemed a little distracted in there."

Beth shook her head. "I'm fine. Just tired, I guess."

Patty said, "I know what we need, girls. A drink. Let's go grab a beer and unwind."

Beth hesitated for a moment, feeling guilty for even considering it. Yet she needed to clear her head and take a break from the case. "Okay," she said, finally giving in. "Let's do it."

As they walked to the nearest bar, Beth couldn't help feeling uneasy. The FBI team was supposed to be helping them, but so far they hadn't made any progress. She wondered if they were even doing anything useful to find Christa and Emily. All they seemed to want to do was block any progress from the Olympia locals.

As they took their seats at the bar, Beth found herself venting her frustrations to Angela and Patty. "I feel like the FBI isn't doing anything to help. We're still stuck in the same place we were before they got here."

Angela nodded sympathetically. "I know what you mean, but they have access to resources and information we don't. Even if they shut us out, they might still find the girls. That's all that matters."

Patty snorted. "They couldn't find their ass if they were holding it. Maybe we need to think outside the box. Try something different."

Beth frowned, feeling like they had already exhausted all their options. "Like what?"

Patty leaned in closer, her voice low. "What if we go undercover? Try to get in with the local trafficking ring? I've done it before and got enough evidence to break up a small local pedo ring in Portland."

Beth's eyebrows shot up. "Are you serious? That's risky."

"I know, but it might be our only option," said Patty. "We could try to find that Hector guy who coordinated the porn movie ring with the coerced teens. If we can get close to him, maybe we can get some information on Christa and Emily."

Angela nodded in agreement. "It's worth a shot. We need to try something different."

Beth hesitated for a moment, feeling the weight of the idea. They needed a breakthrough, and going undercover might be the only way to get it. "Anything to find Emily and Christa."

45

Chapter Five

AS BETH, ANGELA, AND Patty left the bar, their minds were already racing with ideas on how to find Hector. The next morning, Beth and the team began their search. They started by canvassing the area where Shana had last seen the group, hoping to find someone who could lead them to Hector.

As they walked through the crowded streets, Beth was filled with mounting frustration. It seemed like everyone they talked to either didn't know anything or was too scared to speak up. She couldn't help but wonder if they were ever going to find Hector, or if they were just chasing a dead end.

Frustrated and exhausted, they decided to take a break to grab food. As they walked down the street, Grimm whined and pawed in the direction of a street vendor selling hot dogs and drinks.

"Is that what you want, boy?" asked Angela. "I'll buy him a hot dog, if that's okay?"

Beth smiled. "He shouldn't, but he does love them."

Their group headed toward the hot dog stand, and Angela bought a hot dog while Beth ordered a soda. As she waited for her drink, she overheard the vendor talking to another customer about a recent delivery he'd made to a warehouse on the outskirts of town. He was complaining about the ridiculous security measures.

Beth's ears perked up at the mention of the warehouse and the security measures. She leaned in closer, trying to hear more. "Did you happen to catch the name of the person who ordered the delivery?" she asked the delivery driver, trying to sound casual.

The man shook his head. "Nah, just some guy. But I do remember the gate attendant had a really distinct tattoo on his neck. It was a snake wrapped around a dagger."

Beth's mind raced as she tried to think of anyone who fit that description. Suddenly, the street vendor's face lit up in recognition.

"I know that guy," he exclaimed. "He comes around here sometimes. His name is Juan, and he works security for something downtown." He scratched his beard. "Sorry, I don't remember for who or doing what exactly."

Beth's heart rate quickened. "Do you know where we can find him?"

The vendor nodded. "Yeah, he usually hangs out at a bar called *The Pit*. It's a few blocks down that way," he said, pointing down the street.

Beth and Angela exchanged a look, both of them feeling a surge of hope. They thanked the vendor and headed toward *The Pit*.

As they walked, Beth's mind raced with possibilities. Juan might be able to lead them to Hector, and from there, they might find Christa and Emily.

When they arrived at the bar, it didn't take long to see Juan sitting at a table, surrounded by a group of men. They all had similar neck tattoos, but his was the only one with a snake and a dagger. The similar tattoos put her on edge, instantly making her think they were part of a gang. Juan might be the gate attendant, but it seemed like they might all work for Hector.

Beth took a deep breath and walked over to him, leaving Grimm with Angela. "Excuse me," she said, trying to sound casual. "I couldn't help but notice your tattoos, guys." She smiled at the table before focusing on Juan's. "I really love the snake on yours. It's really cool. Where did you get it done?"

Juan looked up at her, eyeing her warily. "Why do you want to know?"

Beth tried to appear friendly and not intimidated by the guys surrounding her. "I'm looking to get a tattoo myself, and I'm trying to find a good artist. I thought you might be able to help me out."

Juan seemed to relax a little, gesturing to the chair next to him. "Take a seat. What kind of tattoo are you looking for?" His gaze was eating her up, and he clearly thought she was there to flirt.

She did her best to maintain that charade while asking about first his, and then the others' tattoos. Channeling her wide-eyed inner ingenue, she made herself sound breathy. "Are you guys part of a gang?" She tried to sound impressed by the thought.

The men around her blinked, and then after a moment, several laughed.

Only Juan looked offended. "You asking because we're all Mexican, *puta*?"

Her teeth clenched, and she resisted the urge to respond that slur. "Of course not. It's the tattoos being so similar."

"Nah, that's just Hector's signature style," said one of the guys.

Juan glared at them. "Clear out for a bit while I talk to the lady."

Beth had a dart of apprehension as they left her alone with him, though that made her odds of taking him better, if it came to that. "I'm sorry if I offended you. I just love your tatts. You'rs is the best. Who did it for you?"

Juan hesitated for a moment. "He's really selective of his clientele."

Beth tried to appear nonchalant. "I want something similar. It's a really unique design."

Juan seemed to relax a little, taking a sip of his beer. "I got it done at a place downtown. It's called *Inked Dreams*."

Beth's heart quickened. "Do you know the artist's name?"

Juan shrugged. "Hector's the owner and main tattooist. Are you really going to get a tattoo? You don't seem like the type."

Beth nodded, feeling a sense of excitement building inside of her. "Neither does my seventy-year-old grandmother, but she got one just a few months ago." A lump formed in her throat, and she rubbed her left inner forearm. Everyone close to Joel had gotten a heart tattoo to remember him. "Would you happen to have any contact information for Hector?"

Juan thought for a moment before jotting down a phone number and name on a napkin. "Here you go. Just tell him Juan sent you but be prepared to pay a high price. He only inks certain people."

Suppressing a shiver, Beth thanked Juan and left The Pit. Angela and Grimm were waiting, and she drove her to the shop, parking a couple of blocks away. Though her car was unmarked, they were being cautious.

She got out, telling Grimm, "Stay," when he would have followed. He looked forlorn as she closed the door, but it was safer to leave him behind.

She made her way to *Inked Dreams*. As she walked in, she saw a large Hispanic man in a white tank top with full tattoo sleeves sitting at a desk, flipping through a magazine. He had a snake slithering around dice tattooed on his neck.

"Can I help you?" He asked, looking up from his magazine.

Beth tried to appear relaxed as she approached the desk. "Hi, I'm looking to get a tattoo. I was told that you might be able to help me out. Are you Hector? Juan sent me."

Hector nodded, evaluating her for a moment before gesturing for her to take a seat in the folding chair across from him. "Sure thing. What kind of design are you looking for?"

"Something on my neck. Juan said I might have to pay a high price to get it."

His expression revealed nothing. "That's a mark of my inner circle, *mami*. I don't hand them out to just anyone."

She trailed her finger up his arm. "I'd do just about anything."

He jerked away. "Not that. I have bitches for that, and you aren't my type."

She'd never been more relieved to hear someone found her unattractive but couldn't break character. "You aren't my type either, but I'd do a lot to get an in with your group."

His eyes narrowed. "My group?"

"The videos," she whispered. "I'm *close* to a guy who was busted at that warehouse near the convenience store. He's been taking care of me, but I'm going to have to take care of myself now, since he'll be in jail."

His lips curled. "What are you looking for here?"

Beth tried to appear innocent. "I was just thinking that maybe we could help each other out. You know, with the restocking."

Hector's eyes widened in surprise. "What are you talking about?"

Beth's pulse thundered in her ears, and her hands were clammy, but she had to press on. "Come on, Hector. You and I both know what's really going on here. I'm interested in making some money, and I know about your side business with the girls, thanks to some indiscreet pillow talk. Maybe we could work together."

Hector leaned back in his chair, eyeing her warily. "And how do I know I can trust you?"

Beth shrugged. "You don't, but I'm willing to take the risk if it means making some serious cash."

For a few moments, Hector was silent, weighing his options. Finally, he nodded. "Okay. I might have something for you, but you have to prove yourself first."

Beth's heart skipped a beat, but she tried to appear calm. "What do you want me to do?"

Hector leaned in closer, his voice low. "I need someone to transport some merchandise for me. It's a risky job, but if you can pull it off, we can talk about a bigger partnership."

Beth's mind raced. This was her opening. She nodded, trying to appear confident. "I'm in. What do I need to do?"

Hector gave her a set of instructions and told her to meet him at a location outside of town the next night. Beth took note of the details and thanked him before leaving the shop.

As she walked out, she felt exhilaration mixed with fear. This was her chance to get closer to the trafficking ring and find Christa and Emily, but it was also a dangerous and potentially deadly job. She needed to be careful, and she needed to make sure she didn't blow her cover. The fate of the girls depended on it.

THE NEXT MORNING, BETH met up with Angela and Patty at a small diner down the street from the station. Grimm was with her, his leash held firmly in her hand. As they sat down at a booth, Beth's mind was racing with thoughts of the upcoming mission. She absentmindedly stroked Grimm's fur, feeling comforted by his presence.

Patty looked up from the menu, eyeing Grimm warily. "You take that dog with you everywhere, don't you? You aren't taking it on the mission, are you?"

Beth hesitated for a moment before nodding. She didn't like Patty's disparaging tone or dismissive way of speaking about her buddy. "Yeah, I am. He's a trained police dog, and he'll be a valuable asset on the mission."

Patty seemed to shrink back a little, leading Beth to believe she might have spoken more forcefully than intended. She eyed Grimm warily. Beth could sense his discomfort and realized he didn't like her.

Before she could say anything, Angela spoke up. "Hey, I can take care of Grimm while you're undercover. He'll be safe with me."

Beth smiled in relief. "Thank you, Angela. I appreciate it."

As they continued to chat, they were interrupted by the arrival of Emily's mother, Maria. She looked tired and worried, her eyes red-rimmed from crying. "Have you found my daughter yet?" she asked, her voice trembling.

Beth shook her head, feeling a pang of guilt. "Not yet, but we're doing everything we can to find her."

Emily's mom nodded, tears welling in her eyes. "She's just a baby. She doesn't deserve this."

Beth put a comforting hand on her shoulder. "We'll find her, I promise."

"I don't know if this is helpful, but I found a picture in Emily's room the other day. It was of her and a girl I didn't recognize. But they looked like they were close."

Beth's pulse quickened. "Do you still have the picture?"

Emily's mom nodded, reaching into her purse and pulling out a small photo. She handed it to Beth, who examined it closely.

The picture showed Emily and another girl, both of them smiling and holding hands. It was Christa. "When was this taken?"

Emily's mom shrugged. "I have no idea. It was just lying around in her room."

Beth studied the picture closely, trying to find any other details that might be helpful. She noticed a small bracelet on Emily's wrist, with what looked like a small cross hanging from it. There was nothing similar on Christa's wrist.

"Did Emily ever mention this girl's name?" Beth asked Maria as she handed the picture to Angela and Patty.

Maria shook her head. "Not that I remember, but maybe her friends at school would know who she is."

Beth nodded. "Thank you for this. We'll look into it."

As Emily's mom left the diner, Beth turned to Angela and Patty. "We need to find out everything we can about this picture. If they're connected in some way, and it seems they are, that link might be our best chance of finding them both."

Angela and Patty nodded in agreement, and they spent the rest of breakfast brainstorming ideas on how to uncover more information about Christa. As they walked out of the diner, Beth's mind raced with possibilities. The photo of Emily and Christa was a valuable lead, and they needed to follow it up.

"I think we should start by talking to Emily's friends," said Beth. "Maybe they know more about Christa and her whereabouts."

Patty nodded in agreement. "That's a good idea, but we need to be careful. We don't want to attract any unwanted attention."

"The FBI?" asked Beth.

Patty nodded. "I can't help feeling they'll just block any lead if we're the ones who find it."

"Agreed," said Angela, looking disillusioned. "It's always been my dream to be an agent, but now, I don't think I want to be part of their team."

As they walked back to the station, she felt more confident they would find Christa and Emily. However, as they entered the station, Beth's thoughts were interrupted by Angela's supervisor. "Hey, Ang, we've received a tip about a possible location for the trafficking ring. We need you and your team to investigate immediately."

Beth listened to the details of the tip. It was a warehouse on the outskirts of town, just like the one the street vendor had mentioned earlier. They had to move quickly. Maybe she wouldn't have to go undercover.

"Got it," said Angela, her voice steady. "We're on our way." She turned to Patty. "You'll have to sit this one out."

Patty nodded. "I know. I'm a civilian." She looked bitter for a moment.

Angela drove, though she didn't use the siren. As the car moved along, she asked, "What's Patty's story?"

Beth hesitated. "I don't know for sure, but I think someone hurt her very badly as a child. She always had a raging urge to go after the pedophiles. She didn't have her badge long before she lost her temper and beat a perp with her nightstick when she caught him actively molesting his daughter."

Angela winced. "That's a tough spot. It'd be hard not to want to beat him, or worse."

"Ironically, a civilian could have done so and gotten acquitted, but since Patty was a professional, she was reprimanded and forced to resign. She was lucky the D.A. didn't go after her. As it was, the sick bastard got a payout from the city."

Angela shook her head. "It's not easy walking the blue line."

"No, it's not. It always felt like part of me though. My dad was a beat cop until he retired. I guess it's in my blood." Beth thought about the times she'd put off Joel for work or the next case. Guilt threatened to eat her alive.

As if Grimm sensed it, he put his head on her shoulder from the backseat, whining softly. She rubbed his ear and turned her head to kiss his muzzle. "I'm okay, boy," she whispered.

Moments later, they arrived at the dingy warehouse on the outskirts of town. They both got out of the car and looked around, taking in their surroundings.

The area was deserted, except for a few stray cats wandering around the piles of garbage scattered around the perimeter of the warehouse. The only sound was the distant hum of traffic on the nearby highway.

Beth clung tightly to Grimm's leash as they approached the entrance to the warehouse. She glanced at Angela, who gave her a reassuring nod.

"Remember, let me do the talking," said Angela in a low voice as they walked inside.

The inside of the warehouse was dimly lit, with crates and boxes piled high on either side. There were a few men lounging around, smoking and chatting, but they didn't seem to pay much attention to the newcomers.

Beth nodded, her senses on high alert as they made their way deeper into the warehouse. Her heart thudded with anticipation as they looked around for any sign of Hector or his cohorts.

As they walked, they heard murmurs of conversation coming from a nearby room. Angela motioned for Beth to follow her, and they cautiously approached the doorway. Peering inside, they saw a group of men huddled around a table, counting stacks of cash. Angela cleared her throat, and the men turned to face them. The closest looked them up and down, eyeing Grimm warily.

"Can I help you?" one of them asked, watching them suspiciously.

Angela flashed her badge. "We're detectives."

The men exchanged a look before the one who had spoken stepped forward. "We don't want any trouble. We're just conducting business here."

Angela kept her tone steady. "We understand that. We're just here to make sure everything is on the up and up."

One of the other men snorted. "Yeah, right. Like we're gonna believe that."

Beth could feel the tension in the air, and things could turn violent at any moment. She put a hand on Grimm's leash, ready to act if necessary.

Suddenly, there was a loud crash from another room, and the men's attention was diverted. Angela took advantage of the distraction to slip past them and continue her search.

Beth followed closely behind, her heart pounding with adrenaline. They made their way through several more rooms, but they still hadn't found Hector or any concrete evidence of the trafficking ring.

Just as they were about to give up, they heard a muffled voice coming from behind a closed door. Angela motioned for Beth to stay back as she approached, listening intently.

Beth could see the tension in Angela's face as she leaned in closer, trying to make out what was being said. Suddenly, the door burst open, and a man came charging out, knocking Angela to the ground.

Beth acted quickly, releasing Grimm and sending him after the man. The man tried to run, but Grimm caught up to him and brought him down, biting him in the leg. As the man cried out in pain, Beth rushed over to help Angela to her feet. "Are you okay?" she asked, looking her over for any injuries.

Angela nodded, her eyes fixed on the open doorway. "Do you hear that?"

Beth eased closer, listening intently. "I wish we had more backup." She could hear muffled sounds coming from inside.

"Same, but I couldn't let Patty in without a badge, and we're trying to be discreet." Angela drew her service weapon again. "Let's check it out."

Without hesitation, she moved toward the room, gun drawn. Beth kept her weapon at the ready, bending low and swinging open the door as she made a wide arc with her weapon. Angela was right behind her, covering her six, while Grimm stayed close to her side.

As she kicked open the door, she saw several young girls tied up and gagged, tears streaming down their faces.

Angela immediately rushed over to the girls, untying them and removing their gags. Beth kept watch, her weapon trained on the door as Angela comforted the girls. "It's okay. You're safe now," said Angela, her voice soothing. "We're the police, and we're here to help you."

One of the teenage girls, with long blonde hair, clung to Angela, tears streaming down her face. "Thank you," she whispered.

Beth's heart ached for the girls, and they had to act fast to get them out of there. "We have to move quickly," she said, her voice urgent. "We need to get these girls to safety."

Angela nodded, her expression grim. "I'll call for backup. We'll get them out of here."

Beth heard approaching footsteps, and she knew they didn't have much time. She and Angela quickly untied the rest of the girls, helping them to their feet. "Can you walk?" asked Beth, supporting one of the girls who seemed to be struggling. The girl nodded, tears still flowing down her face.

Beth and Angela led the girls out of the room, moving as quickly as they could without drawing attention. As they made their way toward the exit, they heard approaching footsteps growing louder. Beth tensed, ready to defend the girls if necessary.

As the group of men rounded the corner, they froze, looking at the girls in shock. "What the hell is going on here?" one of them demanded.

Angela held up her badge. "Police! Get down on the ground now!"

As the men hesitated, Grimm sprang into action, barking fiercely and lunging at the closest one. Beth saw one of the men reach for a weapon and took aim, firing a warning shot. The men quickly complied, getting down on the ground with their hands behind their heads.

Beth kept her weapon trained on them as Angela called for backup, informing them of the situation and requesting transport for the girls. As they waited for backup to arrive, Beth took a moment to speak to the girls.

"Have any of you seen two younger girls named Christa and Emily?" she asked, her voice gentle.

The girls looked at each other, shaking their heads. "No, we haven't seen anyone else here," said one.

Beth felt a pang of disappointment, but they had still made a significant difference today. They had rescued several girls from the trafficking ring, and they would be able to get them to safety and start building a case against Hector and his associates.

As backup arrived and took custody of the men, Beth and Angela made their way out of the warehouse, the girls in tow.

Outside, the fresh air was a welcome relief after the oppressive atmosphere of the warehouse. The girls huddled together, still in shock from their ordeal, while Angela spoke with the officers who had arrived on scene.

Beth approached them, kneeling to speak with them at eye level. "We're going to get you some help, okay? You're safe now."

One of the girls, a young brunette, looked up at her with wide eyes. "Thank you," she whispered.

Beth felt a lump form in her throat, and this was the reason she became a detective. She was here to make a difference, to help those who couldn't help themselves.

As Beth watched the girls being led to safety, she couldn't shake off the nagging feeling of dread in the pit of her stomach. The mission was far from over. They still hadn't found Christa and Emily, and they had to take the next step to bring down Hector and his associates. That meant going undercover.

Beth turned to Angela, who had finished talking to the officers. "We have to keep going. We have to find Christa and Emily," she said, her voice determined.

Angela nodded. "I know, but we have to be careful. We don't want to tip off Hector or his associates."

Beth took a deep breath, knowing what she had to do next. "I'm still going undercover. I'll try to get closer to Hector and see if I can find out anything about Christa and Emily."

Angela's expression was hesitant. "Are you sure? It's dangerous, Beth."

Beth nodded resolutely. "I have to do this. It's the only way we'll find them and bring down Hector and his ring."

Angela nodded, looking at Beth with obvious respect. "Okay, but we'll make sure you have backup every step of the way."

This was the only way forward, but the thought of going undercover made her stomach churn with anxiety. She had to prove herself to Hector, gain his trust, and get closer to him, which was terrifying. Yet she was willing to take the risk if it meant bringing down the trafficking ring and finding Christa and Emily.

Chapter Six

BETH CHECKED HER WATCH. It was almost midnight, and she had to meet Hector. She took a deep breath and stepped out of Angela's personal car she'd loaned her, glancing around the deserted parking lot.

Hector stood next to a black van, a group of men around him. As she approached, Hector turned to her, a smirk on his face. "I see you made it," he said, gesturing to the van. "We're going to need you to drive this to a location about an hour away. There will be someone waiting for you there, and they'll take it from there."

Beth nodded, trying to appear confident. Her palms were sweating, but she had to go through with this to gain Hector's trust.

As she got into the driver's seat, Hector leaned in close to her. "Remember, if anything goes wrong, we'll find you."

Beth swallowed hard, but she had to focus. She started the van and drove off into the night, barely holding back a shriek when she glanced in the rearview mirror and found two men watching her intently.

The drive was nerve-wracking, with every car that passed making her heart race. She could feel the gazes of the men in the back of the van, and she was being watched closely.

Finally, she arrived at the designated location, a deserted warehouse on the outskirts of Castle Rock. As she parked the van, a man emerged from the shadows, his face obscured by a hood. "Hand over the keys," he said, holding out his hand. Her two passengers opened the back door and exited that way.

Beth hesitated for a moment, her instincts telling her something was off. But she couldn't afford to lose Hector's trust.

The man took the keys from Beth and gestured for her to follow him inside the warehouse. As they entered, she saw rows of crates and boxes, and the smell of stale cigarette smoke hung in the air.

He led her through a maze of corridors and finally into a large room with rows of bunk beds. It looked like a dormitory, but the windows were covered with black garbage bags, blocking out any light.

Beth saw the silhouettes of girls huddled in the beds, and her heart ached for them. "What is this place?" she asked, her voice barely above a whisper.

The man turned to her, his eyes cold. "This is where we keep our merchandise. Hector wants you to be a procurer."

Beth furrowed her brows, not fully understanding what the man meant. "What do you mean, a procurer?" she asked.

The man let out a humorless chuckle. "You'll be in charge of bringing in new girls for us. The vulnerable ones. The ones who won't be missed. We recently had too much turnover in the positions, so we need new talent."

Beth's stomach turned as she realized what he was implying. "I won't do that," she said firmly.

The man's expression turned cold. "You don't have a choice. If you want to work with us, you'll do what Hector asks. Otherwise, you're no use to us."

As the man turned to leave, Beth's eyes drifted to the girls on the bunk beds. She couldn't just leave them there, but she couldn't risk blowing her cover. She walked over to one of the girls, a young teenager with tears streaming down her face.

"It's going to be okay," she whispered, taking the girl's hand. "I'm going to help you."

The girl looked up at her, her eyes wide with fear. "Who are you?" she asked.

Beth hesitated for a moment before responding. "I'm here to help. I'm going to get you out of here, but I need you to be patient and trust me."

Just then, the man returned, holding out a set of keys. "Here's the van. Hector wants you to bring him a package. It's waiting in the van."

He had to lead her back through the maze of the warehouse, and she took in a deep breath of the foggy night air, clearing out the disgusting miasma clogging her nose and lungs after being in that filthy warehouse.

"Make sure you get Kayla to Hector in one piece. He's on a tight schedule." He chuckled. "This one is destined for a special live show for select clients."

Kayla whimpered, and Beth's heart sank as she saw the girl tied up and gagged in the back of the van. She couldn't hand her over to Hector, and she couldn't risk letting her go either. She had to come up with a plan, and fast.

She got into the driver's seat and started the van, her mind racing with possibilities. She couldn't let Hector know she wasn't following his orders, but she couldn't let Kayla be taken either.

As she drove, she tried to think of a way out. Beth's mind settled on one possibility. She pulled out her phone and called Angela, quickly explaining the situation. "You need to do a raid on the warehouse as soon as we get there," she said, her voice urgent. "We'll bring in Hector and interrogate him. Maybe we can get some information on Emily and Christa."

Angela agreed, and Beth breathed a sigh of relief. She had a plan, and she could help Kayla and the other girls who were trapped in that warehouse. As they arrived at the warehouse, Beth parked the van and opened the back doors. She quickly untied Kayla and removed her gag.

"It's going to be okay," she whispered to the terrified girl. "We're getting you out of here."

As they made their way inside, they saw Hector standing with his group of men, all wearing the similar neck tattoos. Juan was among them, and he eyed her appreciatively.

Hector looked almost surprised to see Beth and Kayla, but quickly regained his composure. "What's going on?" he demanded. "You took forever."

Beth took a deep breath, trying to keep her cool. "I had to make a detour, but I have the package. Where do you want her...it?" She held Kayla's arm.

Hector nodded, gesturing for her to follow. She prodded Kayla to move as Hector led them to another room.

"Sit down, sweet thing," he said to Kayla with a lascivious look. "Our makeup gal will get to you soon. No need for wardrobe." He gave a lusty laugh that sent a shiver down Beth's spine. While he was busy ogling the girl, she surreptitiously texted Angela, letting her know the location of the room.

Hector turned to her, a sly grin on his face. "You've done well, Beth. I think we can work together after all."

Beth forced a smile, but inside, she was seething. She couldn't let this man get away with what he was doing to these girls.

As they waited, Beth glanced around the room, trying to get a sense of what was going on. She saw makeup and costume supplies scattered around the room, as well as cameras and lighting equipment. Hector's purpose for these girls was clear.

He strode out, leaving a few of his men in the room with them. Beth didn't like the way they looked at Kayla and did her best to shield the girl from their view.

Kayla sat on a stool in front of a vanity, shaking with fear. Beth put a hand on her shoulder, trying to offer some comfort. "It's going to be okay," she whispered. Moments later, she heard the police department's incursion.

Kayla continued to tremble, and she squeezed her shoulder again. "It's okay. Even if they shoot the police, they have good gear. They'll bring everything they have against these sickos."

That brought a small smile to her face, but then she screamed as the door burst open, and a group of officers rushed in, guns drawn. The men in the room scrambled for their weapons, but Beth was faster. She pulled out her gun and fired, taking down one of the two of the men as an officer shot another in the shoulder.

Beth moved to position herself between Kayla and the men, her heart pounding in her chest. Kayla whimpered next to her, and she had to protect her at all costs. "Get down!" she yelled to Kayla, pushing her to the floor.

The men started firing back, and Beth dove for cover behind one of the makeup tables. She returned fire, aiming for their legs to try to immobilize them as the other officers fired as well. It was chaos.

"Drop your weapons and surrender!" shouted a familiar voice. Angela was one of the officers in tac gear. She was clearly hoping to end the standoff without any more casualties.

But the men weren't backing down. They continued firing, and Beth could see the fear in Kayla's eyes as she huddled on the floor, shielding her as best as she could.

The police soon gained the upper hand, and Beth saw several men fall, some fatally wounded. When it was down to two, Angela yelled, "Drop your weapons!" once more, her tone brooking no argument.

Finally, the men complied, dropping their guns, and putting their hands up in surrender. Beth breathed a sigh of relief as the officers moved in to secure the area.

As they took the men into custody, Beth ushered Kayla from the room. She was shaking but physically unharmed. Beth put an arm around her.

As they emerged into the main area of the warehouse, Beth could see the other girls who had been used as part of Hector's operation. They were huddled together, their faces filled with fear and confusion.

They must have been out of her sight when she'd first arrived earlier, because she hadn't realized they were present. If she'd known, she wouldn't have asked Angela to raid the facility, putting the girls at risk.

Beth moved to their side, trying to offer some comfort. "It's okay," she said softly. "You're safe now. We're going to get you out of here."

The girls started to cry, and Beth could feel tears welling in her own eyes. This was just the beginning of a long road to recovery for these girls, but at least they were free. With gentle persistence, she herded the group outside the warehouse and toward a line of waiting ambulances.

As the EMTs evaluated the girls, Beth and Angela watched carefully, looking for any signs of physical trauma or emotional distress. They could see bruises and cuts on some of the girls, and the fear in their eyes was palpable.

One girl, in particular, caught Beth's attention. She was huddled in the corner, her arms wrapped around her knees. Beth saw tear stains on her face and bruises on her arms.

Beth approached her slowly, trying not to startle her. "Hey, I'm Beth," she said softly. "Can I sit with you?"

The girl looked up at her, her eyes wide with fear. "Are you going to hurt me?" she asked.

Beth shook her head, trying to reassure her. "No, I'm here to help. Can you tell me your name?"

The girl hesitated for a moment before answering. "Megan," she said quietly.

Beth nodded, making a mental note of her name. She could see the trauma in the girl's eyes and knew it would take time for her to recover.

Angela approached. "A couple of the girls have to go to the hospital." She scowled. "The EMT thinks one is having an ectopic pregnancy."

Anger surged as she wondered which disgusting filth had impregnated the poor girl.

"We're going to take the rest back to the station to try to question them gently and reach out to their parents."

She nodded, soon easing Megan to her feet to join the procession of girls being ushered onto a bus bearing the logo of a local senior center. Someone at the business must have stepped up to volunteer the vehicle. It helped offset some of her cynicism to know there were still good people in the world.

As they made their way back to the station, Beth's mind was racing. They had caught Hector and saved these girls, but she still hadn't found Christa and Emily. At the station, the girls were given blankets and water while they waited to be interviewed. Beth and Angela worked with the other officers to sort out each girl's identity, taking their statements and making sure they were comfortable.

Once that was squared away, Beth started speaking with each girl separately. The first five didn't know anything, and she was feeling discouraged when she sat down next to Megan and handed her a cup of water. "Are you feeling okay?" she asked, concerned.

Megan nodded, taking a sip of the water. "I guess," she said softly.

Beth took a deep breath. "Megan, I need to ask you something. Have you seen any other girls being held captive? Specifically, a brunette girl named Christa and a redhead named Emily? They're both around ten, and I haven't seen anyone that young in this mess yet." She showed the pictures of both girls as she asked, just as she'd done five times already that evening when speaking to the other girls. Megan was her last hope in this batch of victims.

Megan's eyes widened in recognition. "I know them. They went to my church's vacation bible school last summer. Christa had long brown hair, and Emily had curly red hair."

Beth's heart leapt at the news. "Do you know where they are now?" she asked urgently.

Megan shook her head. "No, I'm sorry. I haven't seen them since then. I can ask around. Maybe someone from the church has seen them." As Megan spoke, tears streamed down her face. "Except I can't go back there. They won't let me in after all this. I'm sorry," she said, her voice shaking. "I wish I could help more."

Beth put a hand on her shoulder, trying to offer some comfort. "It's okay," she said softly. "You've already helped us so much."

Megan looked up at her, her eyes filled with fear. "But what about my parents?" she asked. "What if they won't take me back? And my church...they'll never accept me after what I did."

Beth could see the despair in Megan's eyes and knew she needed to help. She took out her phone and called Megan's parents, explaining the situation, and assuring them that their daughter was safe.

As they waited for Megan's mother to arrive, Beth did her best to soothe the young girl. She got the name of her church and promised to speak with the pastor, to explain what had happened and try to help Megan return to the community.

When Megan's mother arrived, she wrapped her daughter in a tight embrace, tears streaming down her face. "I was so worried," she said. "Thank you so much for finding her."

Beth watched as they walked away, relieved Megan was safe and reunited with her family. Yet her mind was still on Christa and Emily. They were out there somewhere, and she couldn't rest until she found them.

"Beth, look who I found," said Angela, now stripped of her tac gear, with a smile spreading across her face. "I left him snoozing in my office."

Beth's heart leapt. "Grimm, my baby." She hurried over to greet her beloved police dog.

Grimm's tail wagged furiously as he saw Beth, and he jumped up, pawing at her for attention. She laughed, scratching behind his ears and feeling the familiar bond between them. "You act like you didn't see me for years, not a few hours."

"Thanks for watching him for me," said Beth, grinning at Angela. "I missed this guy."

Angela chuckled. "No problem. He's a good boy."

Beth smiled, grateful for her friend and for the comfort of having her loyal companion back by her side. She hugged Grimm tightly, feeling a sense of comfort and safety wash over her.

As she pulled away from the embrace, she noticed Patty watching them with a strange expression on her face. Beth's earlier concerns came back to her, and she wondered what was going on with her former academy classmate. She made a mental note to keep an eye on Patty, but for now, she was just happy to have Grimm back with her.

"What's our next move?" asked Beth as she sat in an empty chair near Angela's desk.

"I'm planning on speaking with Reverend John Crona tomorrow," said Angela. "He's the head of the church that Megan mentioned, and he might be able to give us some information on Christa and Emily."

Beth nodded, feeling a spark of hope. "I want to come with you," she said. "And Grimm, too. He can sniff around for any clues."

Angela grinned. "Of course. I'd love to have you both along."

Patty cleared her throat, drawing their attention. "I think I'll probably head back to Portland soon," she said, her voice slightly subdued.

Beth looked at Patty, noticing the change in her tone. "Is everything okay?" she asked.

Patty hesitated for a moment before responding. "Yeah, everything's fine. I just feel like I've done all I can here."

Beth studied her for a moment, wondering if there was something she wasn't telling them. Before she could say anything, Angela spoke.

"We'll miss you, Patty," she said, giving her a smile. "You've been a great help to us."

Patty returned the smile, but there was a sadness in her eyes that didn't escape Beth's notice.

Beth stood up from the chair and patted Grimm on the head. "Come on, boy. Let's head back to the RV."

As they made their way outside, Beth's thoughts drifted to Joel. She missed him so much. She took a deep breath and tried to push the thoughts away. She couldn't let her emotions get in the way of this case.

Back at the RV, Beth poured herself a glass of whiskey and settled in at the small table. She looked at the picture of Joel on the wall and sighed. "Hey, babe," she whispered, her voice thick with emotion. "I wish you were here. I could really use your help on this one. There's something about this case that feels important. Like maybe, just maybe, I can do some good and really feel like life matters again."

She took another sip of whiskey, feeling the warmth spread through her body. "I miss you so much," she continued, her voice breaking, "But I'm starting to feel like I can handle this. Maybe it's because I have Grimm here with me, or maybe it's because I have a chance to make a difference."

As she sipped her whiskey, she told Joel about the case, going over everything they had discovered so far. Talking about it helped her focus, and she could feel herself getting more and more absorbed in the investigation.

Before she knew it, she had only finished half her drink. She felt a sense of clarity and realized her grief was starting to ease. Or maybe she was just so focused on the case that she wasn't dealing with it.

Either way, she was relieved to climb into bed with Grimm curled up beside her in what was once Joel's spot. She was exhausted, but for the first time in a long time, she felt like she might actually be able to rest. She put a hand on Grimm's side, and the soothing feel of him breathing soon lulled her to sleep.

Chapter Seven

BETH AND GRIMM HAD a quick breakfast, and she was finishing her coffee when a horn honked. Peeking out the blind, she recognized Angela's duty car and waved. She tossed the rest of the precious coffee down the sink and grabbed Grimm's halter. "Let's go talk to this reverend."

They stepped out of the RV, and she locked it before joining Angela in the patrol car. Grimm sat in the back, and Angela rolled down the window so he could put his head out to sniff. The engine roared to life as they embarked on their journey to meet Reverend John Crona.

"How did you sleep?" asked Angela. It could have been a casual question, but she might have guessed Beth didn't usually sleep well these days.

"Better than usual. You?"

Angela nodded as she turned a corner. "Yes. My husband is on a business trip, so it's just me and the cats. I love the man but hate sharing a bed with anyone...except the cats."

Beth laughed as they moved through the city, soon arriving at a church with the sign "First Olympia Baptist."

Angela parked the car, and the three of them stepped out, their footsteps echoing in the empty parking lot. Beth felt the familiar weight of Grimm's halter in her hand, a comforting presence as they approached the church entrance.

Inside, the air was still, and the faint scent of incense lingered. The sound of their footsteps on the marble floor seemed to echo through the cavernous space. Beth took a moment to observe the beautiful stained-glass windows and the warmth of the surroundings. It was a stark contrast to the darkness they had been immersed in during their investigation.

They approached a woman standing near the entrance, who smiled warmly at them. "Good morning. Can I help you?" she asked.

Angela showed her badge. "We're detectives with the police department. We're here to speak with Reverend John Crona. Is he available?"

The woman nodded. "Of course. Let me inform him that you're here. Please have a seat in the sanctuary, and he'll be with you shortly."

Beth and Angela found seats near the back of the sanctuary, absorbing the serenity of the space. The soft sound of hymns drifted through the air, calming their racing thoughts.

After a few minutes, Reverend John Crona entered the sanctuary, a warm smile on his face. He approached Beth and Angela, extending his hand in greeting.

"Good morning, officers," he said, his voice filled with kindness. "I understand you're here to speak with me. How can I assist you?"

Beth took a moment to study Reverend Crona, trying to gauge his demeanor. His face radiated empathy and understanding, yet there was a flicker of something in his eyes that didn't quite match his welcoming smile.

"We're investigating a case involving two missing girls, Christa and Emily," said Beth, her voice steady. "We were told they attended the vacation bible school here last summer, and we were hoping you could provide us with any information that might be helpful."

Reverend Crona's smile faltered for a split second, but he quickly composed himself. "Ah, yes, Christa and Emily," he said, his voice tinged with sadness. "They were both sweet girls. I remember them well."

Beth's instincts urged her to dig deeper, to question his response, but she remained composed, her eyes locked with the reverend's.

"We were wondering if you could provide us with a list of attendees from that vacation bible school," interjected Angela, her voice calm and professional.

Reverend Crona nodded, understanding crossing his face. "Of course, officers. I have that information. Please wait here for a moment while I retrieve it."

As the reverend walked away, Beth felt a growing unease in the pit of her stomach. She couldn't shake the feeling Reverend Crona was hiding something, that there was more to his connection with Christa and Emily than he was letting on. She glanced at Angela, who mirrored her concern. Grimm was visibly on edge as well, with the hairs on his back rising.

"He's not being completely forthcoming," Beth whispered, her voice barely audible. "There's something off about him."

Angela nodded, her gaze fixed on the reverend's retreating figure. "I noticed it too. Let's stay alert and see what he brings back."

Minutes stretched into what felt like an eternity as Beth and Angela exchanged glances, their anticipation mounting. Finally, Reverend Crona returned, a folder in hand.

"I found the list of attendees from the vacation bible school," he said, his smile returning. "I hope it can be of some help to you."

Beth accepted the folder, her fingers brushing against his momentarily. It was a fleeting touch, but she felt a jolt of unease shoot through her. Grimm growled low in his throat when she stiffened. "Thank you, Reverend Crona," she said, her voice polite but guarded. "We'll look into it."

As they left the church, Beth couldn't shake the lingering feeling something wasn't right. She glanced back at the building, a mix of curiosity and suspicion swirling within her. "We need to dig deeper," she said firmly to Angela, her voice resolute. "I don't believe Reverend Crona is telling us everything."

Angela nodded in agreement, her eyes reflecting the same determination as Beth's. "I had the same feeling."

Beth tightened her grip on Grimm's halter, finding solace in his presence. "I'll start by going through the list of attendees from the vacation bible school while you're driving. Maybe we'll find something that will shed light on Christa and Emily's disappearance."

They walked back to the patrol car, the familiar sound of Grimm's claws clicking on the pavement accompanying their steps. The sun had climbed higher in the sky, casting a warm glow over the city as they drove away from the church.

As Beth flipped through the folder, her eyes scanning the names of the attendees, she couldn't help but wonder about the secrets that lay hidden within the pages. Each name represented a potential clue, a thread to be unraveled in their quest for answers.

"Let's start by interviewing some of the parents and the children from the vacation bible school. We need to see if anyone noticed anything unusual or had any interactions with Christa and Emily that might be relevant."

Angela nodded in agreement. "It's a solid plan," she said. "We'll also need to check if Reverend Crona has any connections that could be relevant to the case. We can't dismiss the possibility that he might be involved."

Beth's grip on Grimm's halter tightened, her thoughts consumed by the urgency of their investigation. They began their journey to unravel the truth, driving through the city streets with a sense of purpose. Beth's mind raced, contemplating the various scenarios and connections that could lead them closer to the answers they sought.

Their first stop was the home of one of the vacation bible school attendees. Beth and Angela approached the front door, their badges displayed prominently. The door opened, revealing a worried-looking mother.

"Ma'am, we're with the police department," said Angela, her voice gentle yet authoritative. "We're investigating the disappearance of two girls, Christa and Emily, who attended the vacation bible school last summer. We were hoping to ask you a few questions."

The mother's eyes widened in surprise, concern etching her features. "Oh, my goodness. I had no idea. Of course, please come in."

They entered the living room, where family photos adorned the walls, capturing moments of joy and love. The mother sat down, her hands trembling slightly.

"Did you notice anything unusual during the vacation bible school?" asked Angela, her voice sympathetic.

The mother paused, deep in thought. "Well, now that you mention it, there was something strange. Reverend Crona seemed overly interested in the girls. He would often single them out for special attention during the lessons and activities."

Beth's heart skipped a beat at the revelation. It seemed their suspicions about Reverend Crona were not unfounded.

"Did Christa or Emily ever mention anything unusual happening at the church or with Reverend Crona?" Beth asked, her voice steady.

The mother's brow furrowed as she searched her memory. "I can't recall them mentioning anything specific, but they did seem more distant and reserved after attending the vacation bible school. It was as if something had changed in them. Then Christa disappeared from the church a few weeks later. Emily was so quiet before that it was hard to tell much difference in her demeanor. She's a shy little thing but seemed perhaps more timid than usual?"

Beth and Angela exchanged a knowing glance. The pieces were starting to come together, and Reverend Crona's involvement seemed more plausible by the minute.

They continued their interviews, speaking with other parents and children from the vacation bible school. The pattern began to emerge—whispers of strange behavior from the reverend, subtle changes in the girls' demeanor, and a sense of unease that had settled over the congregation.

"Who's next?" asked Angela after they'd grabbed pastramis on rye from a local deli.

Coordinating with one hand as she fed Grimm a handful of pastrami with the other, she looked at the list. "The Garza family. The daughter is Violet Garza, but it doesn't list the parents' names."

"I know them in passing. Olympia is big, but not so big that I don't know at least some of these people."

"What's your impression of the Garzas, Ang?"

The other detective took a bite and chewed before answering. "I don't know them that well. I think Jose drives construction equipment. Not sure if the wife has a job. I don't remember her name. They struck me as an average blue-collar family."

Angela and Beth arrived at the Garzas' home and knocked on the door. After a moment, a middle-aged woman answered, frowning in confusion. Obviously, police turning up at her door wasn't a common occurrence.

"Good afternoon, ma'am. We're detectives with the police department," said Angela as they both flashed their badges. "We're investigating the disappearance of two girls who attended the vacation bible school last summer. We were hoping to ask you a few questions."

The woman, who introduced herself as Pamela Garza, invited them inside and led them to her living room, where she offered them seats. The room was decorated with religious symbols, including a large cross hanging above the mantle.

Beth handed her pictures of the girls, both separate and the one together. "Do you know them?"

Pamela looked at them, a deep sadness in her eyes. "I recognize Emily, but I don't know the brunette girl. I'm not sure how much help I can be. My family and I left the church a few months ago."

Beth and Angela exchanged a glance, but they didn't want to push too hard. "We understand," Angela said gently, "But anything you can tell us could be helpful."

Pamela sighed, her gaze distant. "The church has gotten steadily more fundamental over the past few years, and the last time we attended, things had taken a turn for the worse."

Beth leaned forward, interested. "What happened?"

Pamela hesitated before continuing. "The organist, Enid Pilcher, started speaking in Tongues during the service," she said, her voice trembling slightly. "It was like nothing I'd ever heard before. And the reverend seemed to encourage it, as if it was something holy."

Beth and Angela exchanged another look. "Thank you for sharing that with us," said Angela, standing up to leave. "If you think of anything else, please don't hesitate to contact us." She handed over her business card.

As they made their way back to the patrol car, Beth couldn't shake off the unease that settled within her. The revelations from Pamela and the accumulating evidence painted a more sinister picture than she had anticipated.

"The pieces are starting to fit together," said Beth, her voice filled with determination. "We need to find Enid Pilcher and learn more about all of this."

Angela nodded in agreement, her eyes focused on the road ahead. "Let's track down Enid and see if she can provide us with any answers."

With their next lead in sight, they drove away from the Garzas' home, minds filled with questions.

"It's concerning how the church's fundamentalism has intensified," said Angela, her voice tinged with unease. "And Enid Pilcher's incident with speaking in Tongues adds another layer to the mystery."

Beth nodded in agreement. "It seems like the church has undergone a significant transformation since the last vacation bible school. We need to delve deeper into this."

Driving through the quiet streets, Beth's mind raced with questions. What drove Enid to speak in Tongues? Did it have any connection to the girls' vanishing? They needed answers, and Enid might hold the key to unlocking the truth.

As they arrived at Enid's home, they stepped out of the car and walked up the pathway, their footsteps muted by the softness of the grass beneath their feet. The front door loomed before them, and Beth took a moment to collect her thoughts before pressing the doorbell.

The door opened slowly, revealing Enid Pilcher, an older woman with gentle eyes and a wary expression. Her presence exuded a sense of serenity, but Beth couldn't shake the feeling there was another dimension roiling beneath the surface. It didn't seem likely to be serene either.

"Good afternoon, Ms. Pilcher," said Angela. "We're detectives with the police department, investigating the disappearance of Christa Stevens and Emily Meadows. We'd like to ask you a few questions."

Enid's eyes widened, a flicker of apprehension passing over her face. "Please, come in," she said, gesturing for them to enter.

They stepped into Enid's home, the surroundings filled with an air of tranquility. The walls were adorned with paintings of religious figures, and the soft sound of classical music floated through the rooms. Beth's gaze lingered on the ornate organ standing against one wall, a testament to Enid's musical talent.

They settled in the living room, a space adorned with warm hues and comfortable furniture. Beth noticed the hint of nervousness in Enid's demeanor as her hands fidgeted in her lap.

"Ms. Pilcher, we've been speaking with individuals from the vacation bible school. One parent mentioned an incident where you spoke in Tongues. Can you tell us more about that?" Angela opened her notebook as Beth held onto Grimm's harness. He seemed cautious but not alarmed.

Enid's eyes darted between Beth and Angela, her lips trembling slightly. "It was a moment of... spiritual transcendence," she said, her voice wavering. "During one of the church services, I felt an overwhelming presence and was compelled to speak in Tongues."

Beth studied Enid closely, her instincts telling her there was more to the story. "Did anything unusual happen during the vacation bible school? Any interactions with Christa and Emily that might be relevant to their disappearance?"

Enid's expression shifted, a flicker of sadness crossing her features. "I tried to be a guiding presence for all the children." Her voice was tinged with sorrow. "I sensed a change in Christa and Emily, as if something troubled them deeply. They grew distant, withdrawn, and it broke my heart. When Christa stopped coming, I didn't know if it was because of her mothers' *peculiarities*, or if she had given up on the Word. Tragic for one so young to burn in Hell."

Beth recoiled at the way Enid so casually consigned a child to Hell. Their version of religion was the kind she hated. The fundamentalist shift of the church, Enid's speaking in Tongues, and the altered behavior of Christa and Emily all seemed interconnected, weaving a web of suspicion and concern.

"Ms. Pilcher, we appreciate your honesty," Beth said, trying to hide her distate. "We believe there's more to this story, and we need to understand what happened to Christa and Emily. Can you think of anything else that might be relevant? Any other incidents or observations?"

Enid sighed, her eyes welling with tears. "I wish I could offer more information," she whispered, her voice filled with remorse. "But I sensed darkness, a sinister force at play. I couldn't put my finger on it, but I knew something was wrong. I fear no amount of praying could ever save those girls."

"You sound as if you know their fate," said Beth with an edge to her voice.

Enid took a moment to blow her nose. "Not their Earthly fate, but their Heavenly one. We must all follow the Will of God and embrace our destinies, no matter how challenging. Christa fell by the wayside, and I fear Emily has too. Their souls are tainted."

"Thank you, Ms. Pilcher," said Angela, her tone cold. She was clearly holding back her anger by a thread. "We'll continue our investigation and follow up on any leads. If you remember anything else about their safety in the Earthly realm, please don't hesitate to contact us."

Enid nodded, a mixture of relief and concern on her face. "I hope you find the answers you're looking for," she said softly. "If not, turn to prayer. God will answer, though you might not like what he says."

Beth and Angela exchanged a troubled glance, their minds racing with the disturbing revelations. As soon as they left her house, Beth said, "There's something wrong with that woman."

"That whole congregation, I suspect," said Angela in a grim tone.

Beth and Grimm walked beside Angela briskly down the street, the weight of her thoughts heavy upon her. The unsettling encounter with Enid made her even more afraid for Christa and Emily's disappearance.

"I couldn't agree more, Angela," said Beth, her voice filled with concern. "There's an air of darkness surrounding that church, and Enid's words only confirmed our suspicions. We need to dig deeper and find out what's really going on."

"We need to widen our investigation," said Beth. "We'll interview other members of the congregation, search the church records, and delve into any connections or patterns that might lead us closer to the truth."

Angela nodded in agreement, her eyes scanning the streets ahead. "We also need to be careful, Beth. This is a deeply ingrained community, and confronting their beliefs and practices might not be well-received. We have to approach this with caution."

Beth's jaw tightened, her determination unwavering. As they got back into the patrol car, Beth's grip on Grimm's halter tightened, drawing strength from his presence. "We're getting closer," she said, her voice resolute. "There's something dark lurking beneath the surface, and we won't rest until we uncover it."

"I think our next step should be to delve deeper into the church's activities and its members," Beth suggested, her voice filled with determination. "We need to understand the extent of the fundamentalist shift and whether there are any other incidents or individuals that could be relevant to our investigation."

Angela nodded in agreement, her gaze focused on the road ahead. "I'm afraid we're dealing with something sinister. Maybe a death cult or sacrifice. I know that sounds dramatic, but..."

"That old lady was just so creepy that it's hard not to let your thoughts go there, right?" Beth sighed. "I just hope we can find the girls before it's too late."

Chapter Eight

BACK AT THE POLICE station, Beth sipped a coffee while Angela spoke with her boss. Grimm loudly lapped water from a paper bowl someone had found him before coming to rest his damp muzzle on her thigh. "Thanks a lot, you drool machine," she said with affection as she patted the dog's head.

He seemed to grin up at her with that uncanny way that sometimes made her suspect he knew more than he let on—and had fun taking advantage of everyone's perceived ignorance of his comprehension. "Your daddy always said I gave you too much credit." She ruffled his head. "Then again, he also thought you were the bestest good boy after you saved his squad."

"What's that?" asked Angela as she returned.

Beth waved a hand. "Nothing important. What did Chief Reyes say?"

"He agrees it's suspicious and is working on getting us a warrant. He has to be a little sneaky, since Agent Johnson is paying more attention to him than us, but he said he'll have it for us by the time we reach the church, so...you ready?"

"Yes." She bent down to pick up the empty bowl and put it in the trash before they left. Grimm moved with pep, like he sensed something was happening. She only hoped he was right, and they were about to make a breakthrough.

The engine roared to life as Angela started the car, the sound echoing through the quiet streets. Beth settled into her seat, feeling the familiar presence of Grimm's head resting on her shoulder. She absentmindedly ran her fingers through his fur, finding comfort in his steady presence.

A short time later, Angela's duty car pulled into the church parking lot. With the warrant secured by Chief Reyes, they approached the church entrance, their badges prominently displayed. Beth's grip on Grimm's halter tightened, her resolve solidifying. They were ready to face the darkness that had permeated the once-sanctified sanctuary.

She could feel the weight of the warrant in her pocket, received, downloaded, and printed from the computer and mobile printer in Angela's car just moments before they reached the church. It was a symbol of the authority they held to delve into the hidden secrets of the once-sacred sanctuary.

As they entered the church, the atmosphere seemed heavy with the weight of the secrets that lay hidden within its walls. The air was still, the soft scent of incense lingering from past ceremonies. Beth's gaze wandered over the stained-glass windows, their vibrant colors casting shimmering reflections across the pews.

"What is the meaning of this intrusion? We're closed."

Beth met his gaze with steady resolve, her voice firm. "We have a warrant to search the premises, Reverend. We believe there might be evidence relevant to an ongoing investigation."

Reverend Crona's voice held a hint of indignation as he stepped forward, his hands raised in protest. "This is a sacred place, and you have no right to defile it with your presence." His protests faltered as Grimm let out a low growl, his protective instincts kicking in. Angela's hand instinctively hovered near her weapon, a silent warning to the reverend.

Reluctantly, Reverend Crona stepped aside, his earlier defiance giving way to a begrudging acceptance. "Very well," he conceded, his tone laced with a touch of resentment, "But know this is a holy place."

Beth nodded, acknowledging his words without flinching. She and Angela stepped into the church, Grimm following closely behind. The air inside was heavy with a mixture of incense and anticipation. Beth's gaze swept across the ornate decorations and religious symbols, taking in the sanctified atmosphere that now held a veil of secrecy.

They made their way through the main hall, the sound of their footsteps echoing through the cavernous space. Beth's fingers brushed against the rows of pews, a silent reminder of the countless prayers and hymns that must usually filled the room.

Their destination was the church archives, where the secrets of the past were stored within dusty volumes and fading documents. The room seemed frozen in time, its shelves laden with the weight of history.

Beth took a deep breath, her eyes scanning the rows of shelves, each filled with aging records and journals. The scent of aged paper mingled with the faint scent of incense that lingered in the air, adding an eerie yet captivating ambiance to the space.

"This is going to take a while," said Angela, sounding discouraged.

"I guess we should get started."

Angela nodded, but she took a moment to place some calls. From the gist of the side of the conversations she heard, Beth realized she was recruiting off-duty cops to volunteer to help dig through the archives.

While they waited for the others, they started shifting through the years of information. With the arrival of additional help, the room buzzed with activity. Off-duty officers joined Beth and Angela, each armed with a determination to uncover the truth. They split up, each focusing on a different era of records, their gloved hands carefully handling the fragile documents.

Beth's eyes danced across the faded ink and handwritten notes as she flipped through the pages of a journal from the nineteen-eighties. She read about sermons, events, and church activities, searching for any mention of unusual occurrences or connections that might shed light on the disappearance of the girls.

Time seemed to blur as the hours passed, merging into a collective effort to piece together the fragments of the past. The sound of rustling pages and hushed whispers filled the air, mingling with the occasional gasp or murmured discovery.

Beth's fingers grew weary, but she refused to let fatigue deter her. Each document, each entry, held the potential to uncover a vital clue, and she couldn't afford to miss anything.

As the day wore on, the room gradually transformed into a tableau of scattered papers and open books. Beth exchanged glances with Angela and the other officers, their faces etched with a mix of exhaustion and determination.

The archaic clock on the wall ticked away, its hands relentlessly moving forward, pushing them onward in their pursuit of truth. Beth hoped somewhere within these archives, the answers they sought lay hidden, waiting to be discovered.

As they continued their search, Beth's gaze fell upon a faded photograph tucked within the pages of an old yearbook. It depicted a group of church members, their faces filled with a mix of devotion and innocence.

As Beth's gaze fell upon the faded photograph in the old yearbook, she studied the faces of the church members, her eyes focusing on Reverend John Crona. Something caught her attention—an enigmatic figure standing next to him, partially hidden behind another person. She couldn't make out his face clearly, but his mocking expression was at odds with everyone else's more innocent devotion.

"Angela, take a look at this," Beth called, pointing to the photograph. "Do you recognize this man standing next to Reverend Crona?"

Angela leaned closer, studying the photo intently. "I'm not sure," she said, furrowing her brows. "The angle makes it difficult to see his face clearly."

"Let me see," said Chief Reyes, who'd arrived less than an hour ago. He seemed a stiff breeze from blowing over and had to be well past retirement age, but he seemed sharp and determined. Beth had no reason to doubt his competency as she handed over the picture.

The white-haired chief studied it for a long moment before grimacing. "That's Ezekiel Kane."

Angela and Beth exchanged surprised glances as Chief Reyes confirmed the identity of the mysterious figure in the photograph. The revelation sent a chill down Beth's spine, and she couldn't help but feel a sense of unease at the mention of Ezekiel Kane's name, though she'd never heard it before.

"What do you know about him?" asked Angela, her voice filled with a mix of curiosity and concern.

Chief Reyes sighed, his gaze fixed on the photograph. "Ezekiel Kane has a history of exploiting people's vulnerabilities and manipulating their beliefs. He has a way of gaining their trust and exerting his influence over them. There were allegations of psychological and emotional manipulation, though nothing concrete to substantiate those claims. He was always trouble from the time he was a boy. Several years ago, he left town, but there have been whispers that he might have returned recently. We need to find him."

"Chief, what can you tell us about Ezekiel's past?" asked Beth.

"As I mentioned, he was trouble from an early age," he said, his eyes fixed on the photograph in his hands. "Ezekiel seemed to have a talent for getting himself and his friends into all sorts of predicaments, and I'm not talking the usual kid stuff. Yet somehow, he always managed to avoid the consequences. I had a few run-ins with him myself, back when I was a detective. The little shit had no respect for the law, but he didn't seem to respect anyone else either. It was as if he operated outside the boundaries of morality."

Chief Reyes continued, his voice filled with the weight of experience. "I'd say he displayed some classic traits of sociopathy, though I'm not qualified to make an official diagnosis. After fifty years of police work, you start to recognize certain patterns. Ezekiel was a master at manipulating others, always staying one step ahead of the law. He had a way of preying on people's vulnerabilities and exploiting their trust. It wouldn't surprise me if he played a significant role in the darkness that has enveloped the First Olympia Baptist Church."

Beth absorbed the information, her mind racing with the implications of Ezekiel's past behavior. It painted a clearer picture of the man they were dealing with—a cunning and dangerous individual who had left a trail of chaos and broken trust in his wake. It seemed likely that kidnapping two little girls wouldn't make him think twice.

"We need to find Ezekiel and bring him in for questioning," said Angela. "He might hold the key to unraveling this entire case."

Chief Reyes nodded, his expression a mix of concern and determination. "I'll do everything in my power to track him down. In the meantime, we can't waste any more time. We need to confront Reverend Crona and get the truth out of him."

As they made their way toward Reverend Crona's office, Beth's heart pounded in her chest. The weight of their discoveries and the impending confrontation weighed heavily on her shoulders. She took a deep breath, drawing strength from the hope they were on the brink of uncovering the truth. The darkness that had plagued the First Olympia Baptist Church would soon be exposed to the light of justice.

Beth and Angela reached Reverend Crona's office, their footsteps echoing in the corridor. The door stood before them, a symbolic threshold they were about to cross. With a shared nod, they pushed open the door, revealing a dimly lit room adorned with religious artifacts and a large wooden desk.

Reverend Crona sat behind the desk, his eyes flickering with a mix of irritation and apprehension as they entered. "Haven't you done enough to taint my church? Must you invade my most holy sanctuary?"

"We must," said Chief Reyes with no compunction as he entered behind Beth and the others. "Don't think I don't remember you runnin' around with that Kane boy, Johnny."

The reverend flinched. "What?"

Beth and Angela exchanged a glance, sensing sudden tension in the room. Chief Reyes's words had struck a nerve, opening a door to the reverend's past the man clearly hadn't anticipated.

"You heard correctly, Reverend Crona," said Chief Reyes, his voice laced with a mix of authority and accusation. "Your association with Ezekiel Kane hasn't gone unnoticed. I remember the trouble you two caused back in the day, leading your little pack of troublemakers."

Reverend Crona shifted uncomfortably in his chair, his eyes darting between the detectives and Chief Reyes. The veil of composure he had worn earlier had shattered, revealing a man who was far from innocent. "I... I was young," the reverend stammered, his voice trembling. "We all made mistakes, but that was a long time ago."

Beth stepped forward, her gaze locked onto Reverend Crona's. "We know Ezekiel Kane has returned to town." Her words hung heavy in the air. "And we believe he's involved in the disappearance of Christa and Emily."

The reverend's face paled, his hands trembling on the desk. "He couldn't be," he whispered, his voice cracking.

"Enough with the lies, Crona," Chief Reyes snapped, his voice cutting through the tension. "You owe these girls and their families the truth. You owe this community the truth."

Reverend Crona's shoulders slumped, defeated. "Ezekiel...he came back a few months ago," he said, his voice barely audible. "He promised me redemption, a chance to make amends for our past. But...but he had his own agenda. I didn't realize the extent of his manipulation until it was too late."

"What was his agenda?" asked Beth.

The reverend burst into tears. "I can't!"

The captain looked irritated. "This ol' boy can answer questions just as easily downtown. The humility of being taken out in cuffs might cure some of his reticence."

Beth couldn't help smiling at the captain's range of vocabulary, vacillating between hick and highly educated. Which was the real captain?

"Beth and I will stay here and sort through his office."

"Good idea, Ang," said the captain as he hauled John Crona from his chair and followed through with cuffing him. The reverend was sniffling like a baby, and Beth was almost sorry she wouldn't be able to see his moment of humiliation. She hoped there was a journalist nearby to capture it, though she doubted that.

Inside the dimly lit church office, stacks of documents sprawled across the desk, evidence of years of congregation activities. Beth sifted through the papers, her fingers tracing the faded ink that chronicled baptisms, weddings, and events held within the church's hallowed walls. Angela meticulously examined financial records, searching for any irregularities or discrepancies that could shed light on hidden transactions.

As they worked late into the night, the ambiance of the office grew eerie, shadows dancing on the walls. The flickering light from an overhead lamp cast an ethereal glow on their determined faces. Beth's brow furrowed as she studied a particularly intriguing document—a list of past church events.

"This might be a lead," she murmured, her voice barely above a whisper. "Look at this, Angela. There's a recurring event marked 'Covenant Circle.' It's not listed in any official church program."

Angela leaned in, her eyes scanning the paper. "You're right. It's mentioned here every few months, but no details, and no descriptions. We need to find out what it is."

The sense of urgency intensified as Beth and Angela exchanged excited glances. The discovery of the mysterious "Covenant Circle" event hinted at a hidden layer within the church's activities. It was a lead they couldn't ignore, and unraveling its meaning could bring them closer to finding Ezekiel and uncovering the truth behind the girls' disappearance.

Beth and Angela sat side by side in the dimly lit office, their minds racing as they connected the dots and pieced together the fragments of information they had gathered. The discovery of the mysterious "Covenant Circle" event had ignited a fire within them, fueling their determination to confront Reverend Crona once again.

"Angela, we need to go talk to Crona," said Beth, her voice filled with conviction. "We have more evidence now, and we can't afford to waste any more time. We need to confront him with what we know."

Angela nodded, her eyes reflecting the same determination. "You're right. We'll bring him face-to-face with the truth and see how he reacts."

Leaving the office, they made their way to the police station, their steps quick and purposeful. The drive downtown felt tense, the weight of their investigation pressing upon them. Beth's mind raced with the evidence they had gathered, the puzzle pieces aligning to reveal a disturbing picture of the church's inner workings, but with far too many gaps to still be confident they really understood it all.

As they entered the police station, the air was thick with anticipation. Beth's heart pounded in her chest as they walked to an interrogation room where Reverend Crona was being held. The door swung open, revealing a small, sterile room with a table and two chairs.

Reverend Crona sat on one side of the table, his face a mixture of resignation and defiance. Beth and Angela took their seats across from him, their eyes locked on his as they prepared to present their evidence.

"Reverend Crona, we've gathered substantial evidence linking you to the disappearances of Christa and Emily. We know about the secret Covenant Circle meetings, the manipulation within the church, and your role in it all." Beth bluffed some, but he couldn't be sure of that.

Reverend Crona's facade of composure wavered, a flicker of panic crossing his features. "I don't know what you're talking about." His voice was strained.

Beth leaned forward, her eyes piercing into his. "Save your denials, Reverend. We have witnesses, documents, and testimonies that expose your true intentions. It's time to come clean and tell us everything."

Reverend Crona's shoulders sagged, the burden of truth finally settling upon him. The room fell into a heavy silence as he appeared to contemplate his next words. The fate of the investigation and the lives affected by his actions hung in the balance.

Chapter Nine

BETH AND ANGELA'S GAZES remained fixed on Reverend Crona. The reverend shifted in his seat, his eyes darting between the two detectives, seemingly searching for a way to maintain his façade of innocence.

Finally, after what felt like an eternity, Reverend Crona let out a heavy sigh, his voice laced with resignation. "I never wanted any of this to happen." His words carried a tinge of regret. "I was weak and vulnerable to the manipulation of Ezekiel Kane. He preyed upon my desperation for redemption, exploiting my past mistakes to control me."

Beth's eyes narrowed. "Tell us about the Covenant Circle meetings, Reverend. What was their purpose? What happened to Christa and Emily?"

Reverend Crona bowed his head, his voice barely above a whisper. "The Covenant Circle was a secret gathering, a group within the church that believed in a twisted interpretation of salvation. Ezekiel manipulated their fears and desires, using their vulnerability to his advantage. Christa and Emily stumbled upon a meeting during the last day of vacation Bible school's sleepover, and Ezekiel saw an opportunity to further his dark agenda."

"What was his agenda, and what did he want from the girls?"

The reverend licked his lips. "I think...he always..."

"Yes?" prodded Beth.

"He always liked to test our limits and make us squirm. The Covenant Circle started to remind me of a game of 'Truth or Dare,' but it was a dare every time. The more people he drew into it, convincing us by facing our fears and doing crazy things, we'd find true enlightenment and God's favor...well, it seemed to feed his power."

"He sounds like a piece of work, but what about Christa and Emily?" asked Angela.

"And you all sound like fools," added the captain.

Beth nodded her agreement.

"He said them finding us was divine intervention. He claimed it was the final sign, and they were brides sent to carry the new vessels that would unite and lead all the people back to God."

Beth almost punched him. "They're barely ten. How could they be a bride or a vessel?"

The reverend was sweating heavily now. "I didn't understand it, but he said to trust in the divine. He let them go, and they went back to the sleepover, but they were subdued after that. I thought he'd forgotten, until a few days ago..." He was openly weeping.

"What?"

"He said it was time to claim our brides. He could sense I was ready to embrace my next state. I didn't want to. I have sons around their ages. I told him I couldn't, but he has a way of making you do things."

Beth scoffed, and Grimm growled. "You mean you're a weak fool, who succumbed. What did you do to the girls?"

"He insisted it had to be on the altar." He looked close to heaving now. "He made me go first. Said I had to consummate to make the child, who would lead us all, along with his brother. Our sons. Our seed would shape the divine."

"Saviors are always men," muttered Angela, glaring at him.

"He wanted you to defile a child on the altar of your church?" Beth seriously considered letting Grimm have a go at him. The dog seemed poised to leap, and his lips were skimmed back. "Did you do it?"

"I..." He began trembling and lunged suddenly to vomit in the trash can.

"Did you?" asked Angela in a hard tone.

He puked again. "I..."

"You'd better answer, or we're going to let Detective Grimm interrogate you," said Chief Reyes. He appeared as disgusted as she and Angela.

"I tried, but I couldn't finish. It was too horrible and not what I believe in." He was in tears and sobbing. "Ezekiel said I wasn't worthy of the gift and took both the girls with him."

"Where?" As she asked, Grimm's leash slipped from her hand. Beth wasn't sure if she let it happen, or if it was an accident. In a second, the dog was on Crona, teeth clamped around his neck, but he didn't bite down. "Answer, or I'm going to tell Grimm to go for it."

"I don't know." He was screaming and soiled himself. "That's the God's honest truth. I don't know."

"You wouldn't know God if he walked over and slapped you." Angela seemed on the verge of slapping him herself.

Chief Reyes cleared his throat. "You two head on out and take the furry interrogator with you. See if you can find Kane."

"What about him?" Beth couldn't even look at the reverend.

"He'll find a nice, cozy spot in a cell. Even that fancy lawyer he called earlier ain't getting him out of this."

"I didn't go through with it," said Crona.

"You tried, you piece of filth, and then you covered for him. He's had those girls for days while you said nothing. You're going down as an accessory to kidnapping, attempted rape of a child, and whatever other charges the D.A. can make stick." The chief gave a cold smile. "You're gonna be spending a whole lot of time on your knees in prison, preacher man, but it ain't gonna be for praying."

That startled a dark laugh from Beth as she and Angela hurried from the interrogation room. "Where do you think we can find Kane?"

As they stepped out into the cool night air, Grimm followed closely at their side, a silent reminder of their determination. Beth looked at Angela, her eyes filled with urgency. "We need to start with any leads we have on Ezekiel. We should try to get as many of these weirdos here in the church as possible," said Beth. "Can your people convince them to come?"

Angela seemed to mull it over. "We can sure try." She was soon on the radio trying to coordinate enough officers to visit as many homes as possible to "invite" the parishioners for a special meeting at the church.

They entered the church once again, but this time with a different purpose. Beth and Angela moved through the familiar hallways, their footsteps echoing in the silent corridors. Their senses were heightened, attuned to any signs or clues that could lead them to Ezekiel Kane.

They began their search in the church records, meticulously combing through the volumes of documents and archives. Beth's fingers delicately turned the fragile pages, her eyes scanning for any mention of Ezekiel or the Covenant Circle. Angela worked alongside her, cross-referencing names, dates, and events. As they worked, people started to trickle in. They kept searching, waiting for most of the congregation to arrive. Emily's mother was there, but not Christa's moms.

She approached Maria and sat with her. "I know you said Emily and Christa weren't friends, to your knowledge, but they must have been. They were playing together at the bible school and stumbled into something they shouldn't have seen."

Maria frowned, glancing nervously at her husband across the room. "They really weren't. James doesn't approve of her mothers' *lifestyle*, so he wouldn't have let them. Christa didn't normally go to church here, but she came a few times with her babysitter, if I remember. The babysitter complained they fired her for exposing their daughter to religion. I guess that might be why she was in the VBS. Emily never mentioned her, I swear."

She nodded and stood up, catching Angela's eye. The other detective was about to spring the Covenant Circle on these people and demand answers. She moved over to join her as Grimm padded dutifully beside her.

Beth joined Angela near the front of the church, her eyes scanning the congregation as more and more people filed in. The anticipation in the air was palpable, a mix of curiosity, confusion, and a lingering sense of loyalty to the church. It was a delicate balance, and they needed to handle the situation with care.

As the room filled with parishioners, Angela stood at the front, her voice projecting with authority. "Ladies and gentlemen, thank you for joining us tonight. We have gathered here to address some concerns and shed light on recent events that have affected our community."

The crowd murmured, their attention fixed on Angela as she continued. "We've uncovered information regarding the Covenant Circle, a secret gathering within your church. We believe it's been used to manipulate and exploit the trust and faith of its members."

Gasps and whispers rippled through the crowd, eyes darting around in disbelief and realization. Beth's gaze scanned the faces, searching for any signs of guilt or recognition. Her eyes settled on Enid, whose eyes darted around nervously, her hands trembling slightly. There was an unmistakable unease in her demeanor, and a flicker of guilt.

Angela's voice grew firmer as she addressed the congregation. "We need your cooperation and honesty in order to fully understand the extent of this situation. We implore you to come forward with any information you have about the Covenant Circle, its leaders, and their intentions."

The room fell into a heavy silence once again, tension hanging in the air. Beth's gaze remained fixed on Enid, her instincts telling her she was the weak link.

Enid shifted uncomfortably, her gaze darting toward Beth. A bead of sweat rolled down her temple, betraying her nervousness. Sensing an opportunity, Beth made her way toward Enid, her voice gentle but determined, though it cost her to try to be civil after the woman's earlier awful remarks.

"Enid, we need your help. We know you were involved with the Covenant Circle. It's important for you to be honest with us," said Beth. "We understand the fear and pressure you experienced, but now is the time to do what's right."

Enid looked down, her voice barely above a whisper. "I... I didn't know what I was getting myself into. It started innocently enough. Just a small group seeking a deeper connection with our faith. But it quickly spiraled out of control. Ezekiel... he had a way of twisting our beliefs and exploiting our vulnerabilities. He convinced us we could truly feel God within if we moved beyond our limits. When I felt the Holy Spirit flow through me and Tongues burst forth, it seemed to validate his words."

"You must have realized at some point he was a fraud," said Angela.

Enid bit her lip. "When the girls discovered our meeting, he was so...he said some things that felt wrong."

"Enid, we believe you have valuable information that can help us find Ezekiel and bring him to justice. It's not too late to make things right."

Enid hesitated, her eyes filled with a mix of guilt and relief. She took a deep breath and nodded, a flicker of determination in her gaze. "I'll tell you everything I know. It's time to put an end to this madness."

She looked up at Beth, her eyes brimming with tears. "There's a hunting cabin on the outskirts of town. It belonged to Ezekiel's father, and that's where he held one of the Covenant Circle meetings. It was something he did to Reverend Crona and insisted it had to be on the holiest of grounds. It's a secluded place, away from prying eyes. I never wanted to go there, but I was afraid of what he would do if I refused."

Angela leaned in, her voice filled with determination. "Perhaps you'll help us save those girls yet."

Enid nodded, tears streaming down her wrinkled cheeks. "Please bring them back safely. No child should ever have to endure what they've been through."

Beth and Angela exchanged a determined glance. They had to act swiftly to save Christa and Emily from the clutches of Ezekiel. Beth stood up, her voice filled with urgency. "We need to gather a team and head to that cabin as soon as we find an address. Time is of the essence."

"Maybe we should call Agent Johnson's team," said Angela. She clearly disliked the idea, since the FBI had spent the last several days shutting them out of their investigation.

"Anything to save the girls," said Beth.

Angela nodded as she reached for her phone and dialed Agent Johnson's number. Her fingers tapped impatiently against the screen as they waited for a response. After a brief exchange, Angela hung up the phone and turned to Beth. "Agent Johnson's team is on their way once we have a destination. I'll call the chief to see if he can get an address from property records."

Beth's heart raced with anticipation as Angela made the necessary arrangements. She couldn't shake off the desperate need to find Christa and Emily before it was too late. She turned to Enid, trying to keep her voice nonjudgmental, though she was secretly repulsed by the woman. "We need you to tell us everything you know about Ezekiel's cabin. Any details, no matter how small, could be crucial in finding the girls."

Enid wiped away her tears, her voice trembling as she spoke. "It's secluded, deep in the woods, but I can't remember the exact location."

Beth's mind raced, contemplating the possibilities. They couldn't waste any time waiting for property records. They needed to act fast.

"Do you have any idea which direction the cabin might be? Any landmarks or distinctive features nearby?"

Enid furrowed her brow, looking deep in thought. "There's a large oak tree near the entrance of the trail that leads to the cabin. It's distinctive, with a twisted trunk."

Angela's eyes lit up with recognition as she abruptly ended her call. "I know exactly the tree Enid means. It's a notable landmark in the area, and we've all—locals, I mean—passed by countless times. You've even been by a couple of times."

"Thank you, Enid. That's a great lead," said Beth. She turned to Angela. "Let's head out now with Grimm. We can guide the teams when they arrive."

Chapter Ten

BETH'S MIND FOCUSED on the task at hand as they hurriedly made their way to the car.

"You drive," said Angela, handing over her keys. "I need to find the spot on the map."

Beth took them, getting behind the wheel. Once they were all secure, she took off in a hurry, following Angela's directions while the lights flashed to clear the way.

As they drove toward the wooded area, Angela's voice filled the tense silence. "I've marked the location of the oak tree on the map. It's a few miles deep into the woods, off the main trail. We'll need to be prepared for rugged terrain and limited visibility."

Beth nodded, her grip on the steering wheel tightening. The weight of the situation pressed upon her, but she drew strength from their determination and the presence of Grimm by her side. She glanced at the loyal canine, his eyes focused and alert, as if sensing the gravity of their mission.

The car sped through the winding roads, the darkness of very early morning shrouding the scenery. Their destination drew nearer with each passing minute. Finally, they arrived at the outskirts of the woods. Beth parked the car in a discreet spot, ensuring it wouldn't draw attention. They stepped out, the cool morning air enveloping them as they prepared to venture into the unknown.

Beth secured Grimm's leash firmly in her hand, the trust between them unbreakable. The beam of her flashlight cut through the darkness, illuminating their path as they navigated the forest.

The sound of twigs snapping underfoot and the rustling of leaves filled the air, accompanied by the steady thud of her racing heart in her ears. They moved cautiously, their senses attuned to any signs of danger or movement.

As they trekked deeper into the woods, the anticipation grew heavier, the weight of the rescue mission pressing upon them. Beth was sure they were on the right track and pushed through even though the darkness and uneven terrain made it difficult to navigate just by flashlight. "What I wouldn't give for a full moon."

Angela's flashlight wavered ahead. "No. He'd see us coming."

"True."

Beth's mind raced, recalling every detail Enid had shared about the cabin. With each step, she visualized the twisted trunk of the oak tree, serving as a guiding light in the darkness. They were getting closer. Surely they had to be, since it felt like they'd been out there for hours.

Time seemed to blur as they continued their journey, the forest enveloping them in its mysterious embrace. The trees whispered secrets, their branches reaching out like gnarled fingers, as if urging them forward and pointing them in the right direction.

"I think we're lost," said Angela a short time later, whispering.

"Maybe. If we had something of one of the girls', I could have Grimm sniff them out." Frustration welled. She was sure Grimm would do what they needed, but without something to scent, he'd be confused.

"Wait." Angela dug in her pocket and pulled out a small ladybug pin in a bag. "This was Emily's. I've been carrying it with me as...well, I guess a sort of talisman, or maybe just a reminder of what's at stake." She removed it from the evidence bag as she spoke, handing it to Beth.

"It might not be enough, since fabric works best, but we can try." She held out the pin to Grimm. His keen senses seemed to detect a familiar scent, and his nostrils twitched as he took in the essence of Emily.

With a purposeful sniff, Grimm's tail wagged in recognition. He gave a low growl, as if acknowledging the task at hand. Beth felt a surge of hope, knowing Grimm's abilities could lead them in the right direction.

"Good boy, Grimm," said Beth. "Lead the way."

Grimm took the lead, his nose close to the ground as he followed Emily's scent trail. Beth and Angela followed behind, her anticipation growing with each step. The forest seemed to come alive, the rustling leaves and distant sounds of wildlife adding to the eerie ambiance.

Grimm led them deeper into the wilderness. His movements were purposeful, guiding them through the dense undergrowth and winding paths. Beth couldn't help but feel a glimmer of hope as they followed his lead.

The minutes turned into hours as they continued their journey, the darkness of the night seemingly endless. With Grimm, they pressed on, fueled by their determination to find Christa and Emily.

Finally, through a clearing in the trees, they caught a glimpse of a dilapidated structure in the distance. The cabin stood eerily silent, its weathered walls telling tales of forgotten secrets and haunting memories. Beth's heart skipped a beat, knowing that they were getting closer to their objective.

"What're the coordinates?" Angela seemed to be talking to herself as she dialed her phone. A moment later, she was conveying the GPS coordinates to someone on the other end. She made a similar call moments later and then hung up. "That's both teams, mine and the FBI, notified. We can wait for backup, or...?"

"We can end this right now. I don't know about you, but the idea of those girls being at that sicko's mercy even one more minute doesn't sit right with me." Beth drew her firearm as she clutched Grimm's leash in her other hand.

"I agree." Angela stepped forward. "Me first."

With Angela leading the way, they approached the cabin cautiously. The air grew thick with tension, each step filled with anticipation and the fear of the unknown. The moment of truth had arrived, and Beth steeled herself for what awaited them inside.

As they reached the cabin's entrance, Beth's hand tightened around her weapon. Angela stood by her side, their gazes meeting in a silent exchange of determination. They were prepared to face whatever horrors lay within to confront Ezekiel and rescue the innocent girls.

With a deep breath, Beth pushed open the creaking door, the sound echoing through the stillness. The darkness enveloped them, but they pressed forward, their flashlight beams cutting through the shadows.

The atmosphere was heavy with a sense of malevolence, the remnants of Ezekiel's twisted influence. They had to act swiftly to find Christa and Emily and put an end to this nightmare once and for all.

Beth's grip on her weapon tightened as she and Angela advanced cautiously, their gazes scanning every corner. Grimm moved stealthily by their side, his senses clearly attuned to any signs of life.

The stale air seemed to close in around them, suffocating her breath. Beth's heart raced as adrenaline pumped through her veins. They had to remain focused and alert, and every moment was crucial in their search for Christa and Emily.

As they moved deeper into the cabin, their flashlight beams swept across the room, illuminating a haunting scene. The walls were adorned with cryptic symbols, evidence of Ezekiel's twisted rituals. Beth's grip on her weapon tightened.

Angela's voice broke the silence. "Keep your guard up, Beth."

Beth nodded, her eyes scanning the room for any signs of movement. The tension in the air was palpable, a silent battle between good and evil. Grimm remained at their side, his presence a source of comfort and protection.

As Beth and Angela cautiously navigated through the cabin, a sudden movement caught her attention. She froze as their flashlight beams converged on a figure standing in the corner. It was Ezekiel Kane, his eyes filled with a twisted mix of amusement and malice.

Without warning, Ezekiel raised a gun, his finger tightening on the trigger. The sound of a gunshot shattered the silence as a bullet whizzed past Beth's ear. Instinct kicked in, and Beth dove for cover, her heart pounding in her chest.

Angela, swift and precise, returned fire, her shots finding their mark. The room filled with the deafening roar of gunfire. In the midst of the chaos, Grimm lunged forward, his protective instincts taking over. He leaped onto Ezekiel, knocking him off balance.

As he fell to the ground, Grimm's fierce grip kept him restrained. Beth regained her composure, her weapon steady in her hands. She approached the subdued figure of Ezekiel, her voice laced with a mixture of anger and determination.

"You're finished, Ezekiel. Where are the girls?" Beth aimed her sidearm at him.

Ezekiel chuckled, a disturbing sound that sent shivers down Beth's spine. "You think you've won, don't you? You're just as foolish as the rest of them. You were blind to the truth, and now it's too late."

Beth's grip on her weapon tightened, her voice steady despite the turmoil inside. "You underestimate us, Ezekiel. We're here to protect the innocent, not just arrest you, and we're not dumb enough to be taken in by you."

Ezekiel's eyes flickered with a mix of defiance and coldness. "You think you're any better? You're all just pawns in a game and easily manipulated. You can't escape the darkness that resides within each of you."

As Ezekiel's words hung in the air, a dangerous glint appeared in his eyes. In a sudden, desperate move, he reached into his boot and pulling out a hidden weapon he aimed at Beth. The seconds felt like an eternity as Beth's heart pounded, her mind racing to react.

Before she could respond, Grimm, sensing the imminent danger, lunged forward once again. His jaws clamped down on Ezekiel's arm, causing him to drop the weapon. Simultaneously, Angela, her reflexes honed from years of training, fired a shot that struck Ezekiel's hand, rendering him defenseless.

Ezekiel cried out in pain, his sinister front crumbling as he writhed on the floor. Beth approached him cautiously, her voice laced with a mix of anger and triumph.

"Your twisted game ends now, Ezekiel. You'll face the consequences of your actions."

Ezekiel's face contorted with a mix of pain and rage. "You can't stop what's already been set in motion. The darkness will prevail." His voice was filled with bitter defiance. "Those fools have embraced all manner of darkness in their quest to reach God." He laughed, sounding genuinely amused. "They'll never be free of my influence."

Beth exchanged a knowing glance with Angela, a silent understanding passing between them. They had encountered darkness before, and they had overcome it. Together, they were a force to be reckoned with. As for the fools in the congregation, he might be right, but she hoped they'd find the courage and conviction to break free of his nonsense.

"You and Grimm find the girls," said Angela, her weapon trained on Kane, still writhing on the floor.

Beth nodded, her focus unwavering. She motioned for Grimm to stay by her side as she cautiously moved deeper into the cabin. Her heart raced, fueled by a mix of determination and concern for the girls' safety.

As she navigated through the dimly lit rooms, her flashlight beam cut through the shadows. Every creak of the floorboards and rustle of the curtains sent a jolt of anticipation through her veins. She called out in a hushed voice, "Christa? Emily? Can you hear me?"

The silence seemed to stretch on indefinitely, but just as doubt crept into Beth's mind, she heard a faint whimper. Her heart soared with relief as she followed the sound, leading her to a locked room at the back of the cabin.

After disengaging the deadbolt on her side of the door, Beth carefully turned the doorknob, her heart pounding in her chest. Inside, she found Christa and Emily huddled together, their eyes wide with fear and confusion. They looked up at her, their faces streaked with tears.

"It's okay, girls," said Beth, keeping her voice gentle. "You're safe now. We're here to take you home."

Grimm nuzzled against the girls, offering comfort and reassurance. Beth's eyes welled up with tears as she knelt, embracing them both in a warm and protective hug. She urged them to their feet and helped them dress by fastening makeshift togas from the bedsheets. "Let's get out of here."

"Please, let's," said Christa, her lower lip wobbling.

As they made their way to the front of the cabin, Beth said, "Don't look at him."

"I want to see him bleeding and in pain," said Christa with a far too adult air of grief, fear, and pain. She'd lost her innocence in every way at this man's hands.

Deciding she deserved that pleasure, Beth nodded to Angela, who came to stand with Emily. "I'll go with you. Don't get too close."

Christa nodded as she stared down at the man who'd been her captor and torturer for days. She spat on him.

Instead of flinching, Kane laughed. "Embrace the darkness inside you, honey. That's what I've been telling you all along."

Christa trembled and reared back as Beth shielded her. She took Christa, along with Emily, outside. She hoped backup arrived soon, so Angela wouldn't have to be alone with the creep for long.

"Officer?" asked Emily, looking on the verge of tears.

"Detective...just Beth, and this is Grimm." She patted her companion, and the girls hugged him. Grimm didn't move from their sides.

"My daddy says you shouldn't hate people. It goes against God." Emily frowned.

"Some believe that," said Beth.

"I hate that man. I want him to suffer."

"I want him to die," said Christa, looking resolved.

Beth wasn't sure how to proceed. She didn't want to say something which would anger the girls' parents, but she needed to acknowledge the validity of their feelings. "I want him to die too. I'm not allowed to kill him, but I would if I could."

That startled both girls, but they seemed impressed. "Will you go to Hell for hating him?" asked Emily.

It was obvious Emily was worried about going to Hell for her own hate. Beth shrugged. As a nonbeliever, she didn't know how to proceed. Finally, she said, "I can't imagine God would hold it against you for wanting someone who caused you such pain to suffer."

"He'll burn in Hell," said Emily with satisfaction.

"There's no such place," said Christa, "But I wish there were."

Beth took that moment to interrupt the discussion by pointing out the sounds of sirens in the distance. Backup arrived soon after, and officers swarmed the area after completing the hike deep into the woods. Officers rushed toward them, weapons drawn.

Beth gently guided Christa and Emily toward the approaching officers, ensuring their safety. Grimm remained by their side, a steadfast presence offering reassurance. Angela joined them a few minutes later, her eyes filled with a mix of relief and concern. "I don't know if I could have stood another minute with him. He wouldn't shut up. I almost shot him."

Despite Angela's half-smile, Beth was sure her friend was being at least partially sincere. "You have more fortitude than me. I would have shot him the first time he opened his mouth."

The girls' parents, overwhelmed with emotions, rushed forward, embracing their daughters tightly. Tears streamed down their faces as they held onto their children.

Beth turned to Angela, a solemn look in her eyes. "We did it. We found them."

Angela nodded, and appreciation laced her voice. "We couldn't have done it without you and Grimm. Thank you for being there every step of the way."

They stood together, a united front in the face of darkness. The aftermath of the rescue operation would bring its own challenges and emotions, but for now, they took solace in the fact Christa and Emily were safe. Beth dreaded the healing ahead of them, but she celebrated they were alive and able to return home.

Beth looked at Angela, a sense of pride and camaraderie filling her heart. "We make a difference, Angela. No matter how dark the world might seem, we have the power to bring light and justice."

Angela smiled, her eyes reflecting the same determination. "Together, we're a force to be reckoned with."

"We are."

"Are you going to stick around?"

Beth was saved from having to answer by Agent Johnson bearing down on them. She seemed intent on lecturing them about their interference in her case. Before she could start, Beth said, "I don't work for you or Olympia, so shut your mouth. If you'd done your job and not blocked us out of the investigation days ago, we wouldn't have had to go off on our own." She looked at Angela. "Come on. I'm starving, and it's way past Grimm's dinnertime."

Angela looked at Agent Johnson for a moment before walking past her. They got in Angela's duty car and drove to a twenty-four-hour diner. A flash of her badge allowed Grimm entry, and they were soon scarfing down food.

Once her hunger had abated, Beth leaned back, giving Angela a solemn look.

"You aren't staying, are you?" asked Angela with obvious disappointment.

"No. I feel like the journey Grimm and I started isn't over yet. I left Denver because I needed to heal and didn't want to be a detective anymore. Now I know that's part of me, and I was trying to excise it as penance for not giving Joel everything he wanted when I had the chance. I'm a cop, through and through. I'm just not ready to commit to one department yet."

Angela nodded in understanding, her gaze filled with a mix of empathy and respect. "I get it. We all have our own paths to follow, and sometimes that means taking time to find our place. You've proven yourself as an incredible detective, and I have no doubt that you'll continue to make a difference wherever you go."

Beth smiled. "Thank you, Angela. Your support means a lot to me. You're an incredible detective yourself. You might take over for Chief Reyes when he retires."

Angela scoffed. "He's going to outlive me."

"To his health, and ours too." She lifted her coffee cup in a mock toast, and Angela clinked against it with her own.

Grimm put his head on the booth, giving Angela begging eyes.

"He must know I didn't finish my bacon."

Beth grinned. "The idea of not finishing bacon is completely foreign to Grimm."

Angela slipped him the last piece, and once he'd eaten, he laid down on the floor under the booth again. "Don't take this the wrong way, but I think I'll miss Grimm most of all."

Beth snort/laughed. "I'm not at all offended. He's the personable one in the partnership."

They sat in companionable silence for a moment, the weight of their shared experiences hanging in the air. Grimm, ever loyal, shifted to rest his head on Beth's lap, his presence a comforting reminder of their bond.

As they finished their meal, Beth turned to Angela, her voice filled with gratitude. "Thank you for everything, Angela. You've been an amazing partner and friend. I'll never forget the impact you've had on my life."

Angela smiled, her eyes sparkling with warmth. "Likewise, Beth. You've reminded me why we do what we do. Don't be a stranger, okay? If you ever need backup or just someone to talk to, you know where to find me."

Beth nodded, a sense of bittersweetness washing over her. "I won't forget, Angela. Take care of yourself and keep fighting the good fight."

They bid their farewells, and she hoped their paths would cross again in the future. Beth stepped out of the diner, the early morning air crisp against her skin as the sun started to peek over the horizon. Grimm's warm body pressed against her thigh provided some heat to offset the sudden foggy chill from a PNW sunrise. She took a moment to breathe it in, feeling a renewed sense of purpose and determination.

The road ahead was uncertain, but Beth was ready to face it head-on. With Grimm by her side, she had the strength and resilience to overcome whatever challenges awaited her. "Come on, Grimm. Let's go home and then just go."

They walked the two blocks to the RV park and were soon in the RV. She was too tired to drive yet, but when the noontime sun was strong overhead hours later, she woke as the bedroom became filled with light she couldn't ignore.

Beth was refreshed and ready to move on. She didn't know where they'd go, or what they would find, but the journey continued, and she was ready to face whatever challenges lay in wait, knowing she wasn't alone. As the miles stretched before them, the possibilities seemed endless.

Meet Izze Prin

IZZE PRIN IS AN AUTHOR hailing from the captivating landscapes of the Pacific Northwest. With a deep appreciation for the natural beauty of the region and a profound love for storytelling, Izze combines her passions to craft gripping tales of mystery and suspense.

Izze couldn't live without her faithful canine companion, Sherlock, who is not only her source of comfort and companionship but also a muse who ignites her creativity. Together, they explore the wilderness, forging a bond that transcends words on a page and infuses Izze's stories with the authentic connection between humans and their four-legged partners.

With a background in criminal justice, Izze brings a unique perspective to her narratives. Drawing upon her knowledge and experiences, she delves into the intricate workings of investigations, the complexities of human behavior, and the pursuit of truth. She explores the depths of the human psyche and the resilience of the human-dog bond through her characters.

When she's not writing, Izze can be found foraging for wild food, immersing herself in the bountiful offerings of the Pacific Northwest. Her passion for the natural world seeps into her stories, creating vivid settings and adding layers of authenticity to the mysteries she weaves.

As a devoted fan of true crime shows, Izze's storytelling is influenced by her fascination with the human capacity for darkness and the relentless pursuit of justice. Her narratives delve into the shadows, exploring the intricate web of secrets and unveiling the truth that lies beneath the surface.

To receive notice of new releases, please subscribe to her newsletter:

IZZE PRIN

https://landing.mailerlite.com/webforms/landing/i4j1m4

Also by Izze Prin

Dogged Detectives
Grimm Pursuit